Building 51

By Jennifer L. Place

Cover design by Erin Kelly

PK Books Inc.

http:/www.pkbooksinc.com

ISBN 978-0-9891177-8-4

Printed in the United States of America

BUILDING 51

Jennifer L. Place

For my father

PROLOGUE

Atop the hills rising from the banks of the Hudson River sits a dormant behemoth; a sagging, ruined bastion to the forgotten horrors and practices of the early era of the mental hospital. The buildings constructed over the vast acreage crumble after years of abandonment, falling in on themselves from rot, disuse and fire damage. Former grand edifices sit as forsaken by the state as many of its patients were by their loved ones.

Initially opened as the Hudson River State Hospital for the Insane, but quickly dropped "Insane" from its title. In its heyday, it boasted one of the most elaborate institutions to shoulder the ever-growing burden of the insane as mental hygiene began to be acknowledged instead of ignored. Staff housing, a power plant, golf course, boat house and recreation building accompanied the facilities erected to house the patients – or prisoners, in many circumstances. The grounds once held manicured lawns where patients could stroll and converse with other residents. Those lawns are now hidden within the overgrowth of the years gone by. Trees sprout haphazardly throughout the grounds as well as on the top floors of patient wings where roofs have collapsed. The fields of the farm once used to grow their food now lay fallow.

Nature is slowly reclaiming the hospital in her silent, eerie way. Vines climb the walls, seeking weak points to infiltrate the interior. Elegant fire escapes constructed of metal filigree crumble into dust where they stand, portions holding staircases to nowhere as their structures continue to fail.

Proudest of all the structures is Building 51, as it was called informally. It was formally known only as The Kirkbride Building. The nickname was drawn from a survey map and the moniker stuck. The original main building of the hospital, its construction took the longest amount of time and funding. It held administration when the hospital for the insane first opened its doors to patients in 1871 and held the bulk of the patient wings.

For 140 years, this tract of land welcomed the mentally infirm, the emotionally delicate, the abandoned feeble-minded, the inconveniences. It was founded and funded with good intentions but for many, its walls held a living hell.

Building 51   1

These were the days when the bizarre and the mundane alike could have one committed. A penchant for tobacco, an abusive husband, or being prone to upset was grounds for a stay. The study of mental health was in its infancy and little was known of cause or treatment. The classifications were broad.

It was not always a temporary stay. Oftentimes, once a patient was processed through administration, they never knew life as a free person again. Mental hospitals became warehouses for human castoffs.

Experimental procedures were performed under the supervision of physicians who were doing little more than playing god with people who were the definition of vulnerable.

This was the age before the advent of the more successful psychotropic drugs, which would be the death knell for this institution and many others like it. The peak population of six thousand residents came just before Thorazine began being dispensed. Following that breakthrough, the headcount began to decline, allowing some who would have previously been institutionalized permanently to lead functional lives outside of a locked ward.

As the numbers dwindled, buildings became superfluous, especially the patient wards. As they emptied, residents left but buildings and their contents remained. And began to rot.

More years passed, more buildings were vacated. Patients were consolidated to other wards but could see the forgotten and neglected remaining, a sad similarity to how many of them must have felt.

Its years of operation were not without controversy. Apart from work and funding disputes, there were the deaths. It was not only the patients who perished there. Staff members met their end, either from patients or suicide or construction accidents. Patients did not always expire at their own hands or due to illness. Some were murdered by the hospital staff. During the first ten years of its operation, the patient mortality rate was sixteen percent; an alarming figure for a facility intended to improve mental health, not a hospital exclusively for the physically ill or infirm.

Some patients simply disappeared. Some escaped and were reclaimed. Some escaped and committed heinous crimes before they could be recaptured. Some escaped and committed suicide before they could be forced back to the hospital. Some whiled away their hours crying or screaming in a padded cell. Some lay still, silent and uncommunicative in hydrotherapy tubs, meant to keep the most violent patients immobile and unable to inflict harm upon themselves or anyone else. Some patients sat upon a park bench on the grounds, ignorant of the beauty around them, because they were drooling from recent electroshock therapy. The landscaped grounds themselves were meant to be their treatment but as time marched on, that concept was forgotten.

For these unfortunates who entered over the years, the road to hell was truly paved with good intentions. And cruel execution.

Doctors naively believed a calm setting, lush grounds and grandiose buildings would ease the internal torment of their patients. When this concept was not the panacea they had thought, they engaged in alternate, often brutal, measures to attempt to return them to sanity.

Several buildings have been the victims of arson, a few of them completely destroyed. Others had floor collapses from the years of disuse and rot to the wooden frame, gaping holes littered with debris that span four floors. Graffiti is found throughout much of the facility, a further insult to its former grandeur.

To prevent further arson and for safety from the crumbling structures, the remaining buildings have been fenced around the perimeter. It deters most, but certainly not all, would-be trespassers from roaming.

The security measures also prevent anyone from bearing witness to the activity of those who remain so many years later, who wander the same halls and lurk in the same cells in death as they had in life.

They walk, they wait, they scream in vain for someone to help...or for someone to hurt.

CHAPTER ONE

The door to the neon and chrome diner swung shut behind Jackson as he shook the raindrops from his coat. He muttered a curse under his breath, pulling off his damp baseball cap. He smoothed a hand over his shaven head, ensuring it was dry. His whiskey brown eyes skimmed the crowd, searching for familiar faces as the restaurant was full to capacity.

A chubby-cheeked young hostess gave him a broad smile, pen poised at the ready to add him to the waiting list. Before she could speak, he raised a finger. "I'm meeting some friends. They should already be here."

"How many in the party?" the girl asked, craning her neck toward the rear corner of the restaurant, which was hidden from full view behind a column at the end of the counter.

"Six," Jackson replied after a moment's hesitation, mentally ticking off their names in his head.

The hostess nodded, smiled. "They're in the large corner booth in the back," she replied, gesturing behind the column. "Enjoy." Jackson nodded his thanks and strode through the maze of people waiting to be seated. He wove his way through the tables to the rear of the noisy restaurant.

The voices of his friends rose above the din of the other patrons. He saw them then, clustered around the table, glasses full of soda in front of them all. Sarah was in the midst of a story or joke, her hands gesturing wildly around her. The overhead lights glinted copper off her auburn hair. White teeth flashed as she began to laugh. The other five people followed into gales of their own at the punchline.

He realized he had stopped moving. Embarrassed, he closed the distance and slid into the open end of the booth, shoving Jay farther in with his hip. Greetings erupted from them all, along with criticisms for his tardiness. Sarah eyed him with mild annoyance, which Jackson promptly ignored. Georgia passed him a laminated menu with a grin. "Don't listen to them," she advised. "They've been shooting the shit for the last ten minutes. We waited for you to order. But decide fast. I'm hungry."

Adam banged his shoulder into Georgia's playfully. "You're *always* hungry."

She rolled her eyes at her boyfriend's teasing. Georgia was all of five feet tall, a slight pixie of a thing, but Jackson had seen her pack away more food than all of the guys on more than one occasion.

Gregory, Sarah and Valerie all bowed their heads to study their copies of the menu. Selections did not take long. They were all creatures of habit and this was far from the first time they had met at this particular diner.

They had begun eating there in college, where they had met and become fast friends in biology lab of their freshman year. They had all stayed local after graduation, a fact which never failed to surprise Jackson. That their circle had remained intact also never failed to surprise him as well.

He was the odd man out now. Everyone else was paired off – Jay with Valerie, Adam and Georgia, and Sarah... Sarah had Gregory, the newest addition to the group; a new recruit since they had begun dating a few months ago, in the wake of her breakup with Jackson. Not that he was bitter. It had been amicable. But the addition of her new boyfriend had thrown off Jackson's rhythm and he was struggling to find his footing as the sole single person among them.

He read over the menu for any changes and, seeing none, settled on his usual turkey, bacon and avocado wrap. Gradually everyone else made their decisions and raised their heads to look for their waitress.

She arrived in short order and they all recited their selections, going around the table. She nodded and departed with a swirl of her ponytail, disappearing into the fray.

"So, Gregory, tell us about this adventure you're proposing," Adam prompted as he raised his glass for a drink.

"What adventure?" Jackson asked, shifting his weight on the bench seat to find a comfortable position.

Startled, Gregory stammered a moment before answering. "Well," he began, looking owlishly at Adam through his glasses, "there was an article in the newspaper recently about the old mental hospital in town. There's a battle going on whether to save it or destroy it and build something new. I thought it might be interesting to do some exploring, if you guys were up for it."

The six of them mulled over the idea. Sarah was the first to speak up. "He showed me some of the pictures online. The place is massive. Super creepy."

"And probably full of friable asbestos," Valerie added glumly. She had majored in environmental studies and could generally be counted upon to be a killjoy.

"Every party needs a pooper," ribbed Jay. Valerie rolled her eyes so far back in her head, Jackson thought she could likely see her brain.

"So what are we going to go there for? Break windows and steal dumb shit like a bunch of stupid teenagers?" Jackson challenged. "I thought we outgrew that after graduation."

Gregory cleared his throat, offended. "Of course not. More of an urban exploration. Apparently there is stuff everywhere – files, patient records, equipment. Just a little adventure to see what's left behind when the state abandons a facility. From what I read, the place had been open since the late 1800's. There's a lot of history there to be seen. I bet there are some amazing shots to be found there."

Sarah smiled at him. "You're never without that camera," she said, reaching up to tame an unruly lock of hair on his head, while giving Jackson a mildly unfriendly look from across the table.

"I would imagine there would be security guards," Georgia mused, obviously intrigued at the idea. "How do we get around that?"

"I'm not sure quite yet," Gregory admitted cautiously. "I'm still working that out. From the little time I've been able to search online so far, it appears plenty of people have been able to infiltrate the site. A group of kids managed to camp out for a few days in there, so there has to be a way in. Give me a couple of days to look into it more. I'll find a way. That is, if you guys want to do it at all."

"What, like you think we're afraid of it?" Jay scoffed. "Hardly. I just have little desire to get arrested pulling a high school prank. If you can find a way to get in without landing me in the back seat of a squad car, I'm in. I love creepy shit."

"Same here," Georgia piped up, and everyone else echoed their agreement. All except Jackson.

"What say you, Doubting Thomas?" asked Sarah.

Jackson mulled it over. "I agree with Jay on being able to avoid arrest. My employer frowns on that. So if you've got a plan to keep us all out of jail, I guess I'm in."

Gregory grinned with satisfaction. "I'll figure it out and do some further research and then we'll discuss it further and decide when to go in."

The group nodded their assent as the waitress arrived with their food. The conversation turned to light banter as they ate.

After the check had been argued over, split between them and paid, they all walked out to the parking lot together. The rain had tapered to a light mist that made the cars glitter under the street lamps. Jackson brought up the rear and noticed Sarah lagging from the group. He caught up to her and they paced each other as they crossed the lot to their cars.

"Cut Gregory some slack," she said, not unkindly. "He's still new to all of you; he doesn't have the benefit of history with everyone. I think he very much wants you all to accept him. You most of all."

"Me?" Jackson retorted, incredulous. "Why would he care if I accept him?"

She sighed in response. "Because you and I were together and now we're not, but you're still my friend. And he knows I would hate it if he went all alpha male weirdo about you. So just lighten up a little, would ya?"

She kissed him gently on the cheek and darted off to her own car, where Gregory was waiting for her at the passenger door. She unlocked the doors for him, the orange lights illuminating the wet pavement, and got in as well, leaving Jackson to scowl alone in the parking lot.

CHAPTER TWO

Two weeks passed before the troupe of friends met up again, this time for beers at Sarah's apartment.

Jackson was early this time, avoiding the ribbing he had received at the diner. His knock on her door was met with a loud instruction to enter. He found Sarah alone, hunched before an open refrigerator putting bottles of beer inside. Jackson walked into the tiny kitchen, just off the living room, and placed the six-pack of Newcastle he had brought next to the others on the floor.

"You know, you probably shouldn't invite every yahoo who knocks on your door into your apartment," he admonished.

She didn't turn her head or pause in her task. "The only yahoos I'm expecting, or that knock on my door, are you guys," she responded with a heavy dose of sarcasm. With a finger, she dragged his six-pack closer to her and began placing them alongside the other bottles inside the refrigerator. "If you wouldn't mind helping a lady out, you could put those chips into bowls and set them out for me." She gestured toward several bags on top of the small kitchen table. "You know where the bowls are."

He nodded and crossed to the other side of the room, pulling a few dollar-store plastic bowls from the cabinet. Placing the bowls on the table, he inspected the bags.

"Bugles. I'm touched," he remarked, laughing, as he tore open the package and poured them into a smaller bowl.

"I know they're your favorite," Sarah replied, and Jackson could hear the smile in her voice. "I remember everyone's favorites. Junk food consumption is key to any meaningful friendship."

"There is truth in that," Jackson agreed, watching cheese curls cascade from a bag, orange powder coating the counter. He wiped it up absently with his hands and then brushed them together. "Is everyone coming?"

Sarah stood up, closing the refrigerator door. "Supposed to be, yes. Help me break these down for recycling." She thrust the six-pack carriers at him unceremoniously.

He rolled his eyes but did as she asked. As he was folding the second carrier, a series of fast raps sounded at the door. Sarah shouted the same command she had given Jackson as she carried the bowls of chips into the living room.

Gregory entered the apartment, bookish and seemingly uncomfortable as always. He eyed Jackson uneasily; leery of the fact he had arrived first.

Attempting to put him at ease, Jackson decided to put more of an effort into being friendly. "Gregory," he said, nodding his head at the other man. "Nice to see you again."

"Uhh...nice to see you too," Gregory agreed, though he sounded unconvinced, pushing his glasses higher on the bridge of his nose. He, like Jackson, had not come empty handed.

They were all young and not overpaid, and beer was a necessity. Everyone contributed toward community booze when they all got together. It was an unspoken rule. If you couldn't afford a six-pack, you at least sprung for a two dollar bag of tortilla chips and some salsa. Gregory had caught on quickly when he and Sarah had begun dating.

Sarah kissed the corner of Gregory's mouth in greeting. "Can you put those in the fridge for me?"

Gregory wandered into the kitchen, following orders. It was rare for someone to balk at Sarah's requests. She wasn't a mean girl, per se; it was more that she possessed a strong and sometimes overbearing personality. It was mostly endearing and those around her generally did as she said. Gregory was no different, Jackson noticed.

"I guess I get to give everyone else shit for being late this time," Jackson joked, seating himself on a bean bag chair near the rear corner of the room. Sarah's apartment was an odd assortment of furniture, spider plants, and bookcases. It was as eclectic as its tenant. Books were everywhere, spilling out of the shelves and occupying space on the coffee table, TV stand, the floor, and the arm of the couch. They ranged in subject from religion to the civil war to romance to computer programming. Sarah was a web developer and she had various and sundry geek bibles throughout the apartment for work.

Jackson chided himself internally for not grabbing a beer for himself before sitting down. Once ensconced within a bean bag chair, it was next to impossible to extract yourself without a shoehorn or pulley system. He would simply have to wait until the others arrived and prey upon their mercy to get one for him. He was not about to make such a request of Sarah or Gregory.

"They should be here soon," Sarah told him, curling up on the corner of her faded denim couch, tucking her bare feet underneath her. "Georgia texted me just before you got here to say they were on their way." Gregory sat down next to Sarah, handing her a beer and placing his own on a coaster on the coffee table.

Jackson was relatively sure he had never met anyone quite as fastidious before. The man was wrapped so tight his nerves must be ready to scream. The disparity between their personalities bewildered Jackson; he could not understand how Sarah went from dating him to dating Gregory. They could not have been more opposite. It wasn't just the physical characteristics – Jackson was more burly and with a shaved head while Gregory had more of a slender, owlish appearance, not to mention that he had hair; but the core of their personalities. Jackson carried himself with an easy confidence and was lightning fast to crack a joke or to put someone at ease. Gregory always had a look of confusion on his face when someone made a joke, as if he didn't understand humor at all. Jackson saw him as being a man out of time, out of place in almost any situation that involved other people. His natural habitat would likely be the back room of a library.

Yet again, knuckles sounded upon the door, loud voices making a ruckus behind it. They did not wait to be told to enter, and, laughing, the foursome stumbled into the apartment, bearing more beer and snacks.

"Hey hey, the gang's all here," Jay crowed, taking the bags of chips from Adam's hands and placing them on the kitchen table.

"So it appears," Sarah said wryly, eyeing them over her beer. "Just put the beer on the table. The fridge is full."

"Aye, Captain," Georgia giggled with a mock salute. She disappeared briefly into the kitchen.

"Hey G, could you grab me a beer while you're in there? I'm never going to be able to get out of this chair," Jackson called, straining a bit to be heard over the din.

"Surely. Just hope you don't have to pee," Georgia answered. She emerged a moment later, two long-necked bottles in her hands. She passed one to Jackson and then took a seat on the floor between him and the television, snagging one of the overstuffed throw pillows Sarah had scattered throughout the living room.

Adam reclined in the wicker framed papasan chair in the opposite corner, like a king on a creaking throne. "So...what's the news on the nuthouse adventure?" It took him a few minutes of shifting to find a position which didn't make him feel like he was about to topple over.

Gregory choked on his mouthful of beer, Sarah playfully slapping him on the back. "Well," he began, after he had cleared his throat, "I found a way in that shouldn't be too difficult. It'll take a bit of a hike to get there, though. Hope no one minds that much."

"Are you casting aspersions about our athleticism?" Valerie joked from the kitchen, where she was rummaging through Sarah's refrigerator, in search of a jar of salsa.

"Of course not," Gregory retorted. "I wasn't sure how all in everyone was. The site itself is enormous, so I wanted to be clear on how much it would entail to get there as well as the actual exploring."

"I think we'll all be fine," Jay assured him, grinning.

"All right then," Gregory said, mollified. "There's a side road by the gas station. It leads up to the American Legion building, which is not far from the hospital's old power plant. From what I've found, there's an entry point in the fence near the plant and we can get onto the grounds from there."

"That's great that you found that," Jackson began to say.

"Ah, Doubting Thomas strikes again," Sarah interrupted.

"Now hold on a second," Jackson rebutted, getting impatient. "If you'd have let me finish, I was merely going to ask where we were supposed to leave our cars while we're doing this. We can't only take one, and it would be too obvious to leave them at the Legion. No one wants to get towed or make it look like we've broken into the hospital."

Gregory glanced at Jackson with new respect. "Excellent point. I've given that some thought. We don't want to get caught before we even get in and we also don't want to come back out without a way to get home." He took a pull from his drink before continuing.

He's really enjoying this, Jackson thought, with an internal eye roll. He mentally patted himself on the back for asking his question with less irritation than he felt.

"There's a kid who works at the gas station who I used to tutor. I ran into him there yesterday after I took a drive up to the Legion building to check it out. I mentioned to him that I was thinking of trying to check out the hospital but wasn't sure of the logistics for getting in and leaving my car. He told me it wouldn't be a problem to park in the station lot, so long as it was a day he was working. He said he would make sure we didn't get towed." Gregory smiled at Sarah with satisfaction.

"Well, hold on a minute," Jay declared, raising a finger. "What time of day were you thinking to start this trek? Because if we're going in the daytime, isn't it a bit suspicious for seven people trudging up a side road toward a known point of interest for trespassing?"

"And if we're going at night," Georgia continued, taking up the thread as she dipped a chip into a bowl of salsa, "we aren't going to have any idea where the hell we are in there. It's not as if we have the right gear for this. I certainly don't have a set of night vision goggles to bring along with me and I doubt my app for driving directions is going to be much help."

Gregory appeared instantly deflated at the dissension. "I hadn't considered it from that perspective," he admitted, clearly relying on theoreticals and not execution.

Valerie piped up. "Problem solved. My grandmother lives a few doors down from the Legion hall. Remember? We can park there."

"Why the hell did you wait until now to mention that?" Sarah asked, annoyed.

Valerie shrugged. "I wanted to see if anyone had any better ideas."

"Oh good god," Sarah exclaimed, throwing her hands in the air.

"You could have thought of that too," Valerie countered. "It's not like you've never been there before."

"What are you going to tell her we're parking there for?" Adam asked.

"Exactly what we're parking there for," Valerie answered, matter-of-factly. "Honestly, she probably has stories about that place. Her father worked there when she was growing up, I think. She knows people go in there and since she lives on that street and she's a total busybody, she more than likely knows if and when the street is patrolled."

"Well, that certainly takes care of that," Jackson remarked. He cast a grin at Valerie, who winked at him. She was not much of a Gregory fan either, and had been disappointed when Jackson and Sarah had broken up.

"I guess the only other detail to work out is when we want to do this," Gregory noted.

"I vote for going in during the daytime," Jay suggested. "We'll at least be able to get a sense of the layout if we have a couple hours of light."

There were murmurs of agreement among the others. "I agree," Gregory responded. "I'm guessing either a Saturday or Sunday afternoon would be best, given our work schedules."

More nods and agreement. "How many buildings are we talking here?" Jackson asked.

Gregory thought for a moment. "In total or the larger buildings?"

"Both, I suppose. I don't know a damn thing about this place," Jackson answered.

Adam answered him. "At least seventy total, probably more. In addition to the main buildings, there were cottages for the staff that lived on site."

Surprised, Jackson turned to look at him. "How do you know?"

"I harnessed the power of the internet," Adam explained simply. "Didn't you look it up after the diner?"

"It never occurred to me," Jackson acknowledged.

"I figured most of you would have, at least briefly," Gregory concurred, surprised Jackson hadn't looked it up. The others nodded in agreement.

Jackson felt sheepish and the tiniest bit of unease began to circulate through him. Why hadn't he looked it up? It wasn't as if he didn't have down time at his job to do a cursory search on the hospital or its layout and history. He worked for a property management company and his position had afforded him the opportunity to become a master at computer solitaire.

"I really want to check out the morgue," Georgia chimed in, excitement in her voice.

"You're so morbid," Sarah retorted, looking a bit green around the gills at the suggestion.

"There's a morgue?" Jackson blurted.

"Of course there's a morgue, dummy," Georgia laughed. "It *was* a hospital. People die in hospitals."

"And apparently a *lot* of them died at this one," Valerie agreed, brown eyes gleaming. Their excitement was tangible. "They didn't just have the insane, they had several tuberculosis hospitals. Those people never left. Once you got that, you basically went there to die."

Gregory nodded in agreement. "And from the statistics I've found, the death rate was significant for the staff as well as the patients."

"Fabulous," Jackson muttered, finishing off his beer.

"Scared?" Sarah sneered.

"No, Sarah, I am not scared," Jackson answered through gritted teeth. "But the idea of traipsing through failing buildings that are falling apart and are probably full of lead paint and asbestos that held legions of the crazy and ill that all perished there…well, Disney World it ain't."

"No, Disney World is far more terrifying," Jay snickered. "All those snot-nosed kids and their asshole parents? I'll take my chances with the crazies."

They all laughed, filled with the arrogance of youth, none of them yet feeling any tempting pull of parental urges. The seven of them still believed themselves immortal and untouchable.

Only Jackson's laugh was half-hearted. He was curious about the place, sure. There was no sense of excitement or anticipation, only a seed of dread taking root in his chest at the thought of entering those grounds.

CHAPTER THREE

"I think it's the yellow one up there," Sarah told Jackson, who was navigating his car at a painfully slow pace up the residential street in search of Valerie's grandmother's house.

"I thought it was number forty-two," Jackson argued.

"She totally said it was yellow," Sarah protested, craning her neck to look up the street through the windshield. Her seatbelt pulled taut and she strained against it.

"I don't remember her mentioning a color," Gregory said doubtfully from his position in the back seat. "How do you not know which one it is? You've actually been there!"

"Valerie always drove," Sarah replied, sullen.

"See? Someone agrees with me," Jackson exclaimed. "Or we could just look for Valerie's car in the driveway."

Sarah grunted and flung herself dramatically back against the seat. "There you go being logical again."

"So sorry," Jackson apologized, his tone dripping with sarcasm. He could have sworn he had heard Gregory snicker from the seat behind Sarah. Maybe he wasn't so bad after all, Jackson thought to himself, as he scanned the driveways ahead of him.

The street was narrow and well maintained. The houses on either side were 1950's ranch style, most with brick facades. After living in the area for a while, Jackson had noticed there were quite a number of neighborhoods – or developments, as they were mainly referred to here – built on cul de sacs where the houses were all carbon copies of one another in the fashion of a bygone era.

When the main employer in the area, a computer company, had made cutbacks, it had an enormous impact on the local economy and few of the houses in the outlying towns had seen many updates that were not necessities. There was some new construction of the high-end "McMansion" style for those in the higher income bracket who wanted to escape the confines of New York City or Westchester County, but the majority of residents were blue collar.

Jackson glanced at the cars in the driveways, spotting Valerie's rust bucket up on his left. "There we are," he announced, putting on his directional to turn in. He pulled in behind her car and put his in park. Sarah and Gregory were out of the car before he had even unlatched his seatbelt and were headed for the front door. Valerie stood in the doorway, clad in jeans, sturdy hiking boots and a faded Greenpeace t-shirt.

"Took you long enough," she told them, holding the door open for them to enter.

"There was a bit of a disagreement on the house's location," Gregory told her, ducking his head through the entryway.

"Really? I told you it was number forty-two. The number is pretty visible," Valerie responded.

"Jackson thought it was yellow," Sarah commented, swallowing a laugh.

He sputtered angrily as he passed last through the open screen door, which slapped loudly behind him. "I never said it was yellow," Valerie mused, puzzled.

"That's what I told him!" Sarah exclaimed.

"You're hilarious," Jackson snarled. "So when's your first open mic night at the comedy club?"

Adam, Jay and Georgia were all seated around a large Formica kitchen table along with a tiny older woman, obviously Valerie's grandmother. All but the grandmother had dressed appropriately for the journey in jeans and boots. Georgia, as usual, was sporting her practical punk look and had elected to represent with a Ramones shirt. Everyone else was tame in comparison.

"Well, Val, I suggest you introduce me to this straggler here," the old woman said. She was old, but not ancient; her hair a steely gray and had friendly, brown eyes surrounded by folds and creases that appeared as delicate as tissue paper. She was small without appearing frail. Personality emanated from her as she greeted them with a smile.

"Gram, this is Gregory," Valerie told her, exasperated by the formal gesture.

"Make yourself at home. And please, either call me Gram or Louise. None of that 'Mrs. Hood' business. Makes me feel old." She gestured to empty chairs opposite her at the table. "Have a seat. I won't keep you all from whatever it is you're doing. What is it you're doing, anyway? Am I aiding and abetting by allowing you to park your getaway cars on my property?"

Gregory looked pained. "No, ma'am…"

"A potential high speed chase? Spot on the evening news, perhaps?"

Valerie rolled her eyes at her grandmother. "No, Gram. None of that. And I'm not sure if you've seen my car lately, but it's not going to be in any high speed chase."

"That's disappointing. Nothing exciting happens on this damn street except for those idiot kids across the road occasionally falling out of a tree."

"Sorry we aren't more exciting," Adam apologized, his lips tugging up into a grin.

"So what *are* you planning?" Louise asked again.

"We're going to survey the hospital," Gregory explained. "We were planning to access the grounds near the power plant."

"Oh, that place," Louise said disgustedly. "Why on earth would you want to do that?"

"Lots of people have gone there, Gram," Valerie argued. "Like, why do you think they put a fence up?"

"Oh, I don't know, young lady. Maybe because idiot kids – older versions of the ones across the street, probably – went in there and did drugs and spray painted everything and set fire to parts of it. Those buildings are all falling apart. It's not safe in there at all," the old woman scolded.

Gregory's face was solemn. "Well, ma'am…"

"Stop calling me ma'am. That is just as bad."

"Fair enough. Well, Louise, I have a pretty good idea from the research I've done which areas to steer clear. We aren't looking to desecrate the site further, or do drugs, or set fires, as you mentioned. This is more to see what's left."

Louise shuddered. "Never did like that place. Gave me the willies. When it was open, years back, if the wind was blowing the right way, you could hear some of them screaming over there."

When six sets of eyes looked at her with astonishment, Valerie spoke up again. "Oh, that's nonsense, Gram. Guys don't listen to her. She's just messing with you."

"I am not, Valerie Ann. There's been a time or two since it's been closed that I've heard it as well."

"Your hearing must be failing, then," her granddaughter retorted. "There's no one there anymore."

"It could have been those idiot kids you mentioned," Georgia suggested playfully.

"I suppose it could have been. Open or closed, it's a creepy place. Even when it was younger and beautiful. Still creeped me out. A lot of bad happened there."

Gregory's ears perked at that. "Do you have any stories you'd like to share about it, Louise?" he inquired, hopeful.

The old woman waved him off. "No, I never spent much time there. As little as possible, really. My father worked there. It was the biggest employer in the area back then. We didn't live in the staff housing like many families employed there, and I'm glad for that. No, I don't have any stories to tell you. Just that my daddy came home at night on more than one occasion with a haunted look in his eyes and he tried to never talk about that place."

"Understood," Gregory replied.

"Val, I really don't like this idea at all," Louise told her, staring directly at her granddaughter from across the table. Her expression was grave. "It's dangerous."

"Your objections have been noted and overruled, Gram," Valerie answered, her face equally as serious. Jackson watched the two women, seeing not only the physical similarity but also in their character.

She nodded, acknowledging her defeat. "Now then," Louise spoke again, her voice brighter. "It's not a short walk to get there from here. You'll need to go through the woods from my backyard to get to the power plant. Stay on a pretty straight course and it'll get you there. Do you have supplies with you?"

Jay pointed to the backpacks lined up along the floor in the living room. "We have flashlights and bottles of water, some granola bars, a set of bolt cutters, and a first aid kit."

Louise nodded. "You did well to wear jeans. There are a lot of pricker bushes in those woods. You'll want bug spray. Val, there should be some in the hall closet. Take that, too." Valerie nodded and left the room, following orders. "Take a few minutes to charge up your phones before you go. I'll make you some sandwiches so you aren't exploring on empty stomachs."

"That's very nice, but you don't have to do that," Georgia protested, not wanting to put her out.

"Nonsense. It's my pleasure," Louise informed her. "But I'll let you help me so your conscience is clear."

Georgia immediately rose from her seat. "I am at your command."

"If only," Louise laughed. "I'd have had you come earlier and had you clean the windows and mow the lawn."

"I'm really more of a sandwiches girl," Georgia assured her. "I'm more eating than hard labor."

"It's true," the others agreed in chorus.

Georgia glared at them all with only a little malice. "Sandwiches are my favorite food," she confessed to Louise conspiratorially.

"Mine too, girl," Louise agreed, and slapped a package of sliced bread into Georgia's hand. "So let's make some good ones."

CHAPTER FOUR

They set out after helping Louise with the dishes despite her many protests that their help was unnecessary. The afternoon was bright and cool for late spring, assisted by the canopy of trees surrounding them. Gregory led the way, pushing through the low brush, compass in hand. There was little sound aside from that of their feet pushing through the deadfall.

After half an hour's trek, they noticed the trees begin to thin out and the smoke stack to the power plant emerged before them. Gregory turned to look at the others, face flushed with excitement as well as exertion.

"Almost there," he informed them, pocketing the compass.

"Thank god," Sarah muttered. "I think my shins are covered in burrs." She stopped walking as she reached the end of the tree line to pull the loathsome, prickly brown balls from her jeans.

"Seriously," Valerie agreed, checking her legs as well.

Jackson stopped alongside the girls, getting his first good look at the power plant and the high fence surrounding it. The plant was an expansive brick building, much like the majority of all of the other structures belonging to the hospital. The one differentiating feature was the smoke stack, which towered over them, seeming to touch the sky. The outer walls of the building were covered with graffiti, a sight which would quickly become familiar to them. Windows were broken; debris littered the ground surrounding the building. The grass was overgrown and full of tall weeds and bushes. Ivy climbed around the front entrance.

"It's really something," Jackson opined, eyes scanning for any evidence of other people in sight.

"You haven't seen anything yet," Gregory assured him. He slung his backpack from his shoulders, rummaging inside and extracting the smallest bolt cutter Jackson had ever seen.

"Do you do a lot of this?" Jackson asked, curious about the sophisticated equipment for such a studious young guy. The cutters couldn't have been cheap.

"Rich parents," Sarah told Jackson, taking a swig from one of her bottles of water.

Gregory nodded absently. "Yup."

Adam and Jay had walked ahead of them to the fence, inspecting it for existing entry points.

"I hope you kept the receipt," Jay said, pulling back a section of fence that someone before them had cut loose. "Looks like we won't need your fancy clippers."

"Looks like security isn't super diligent," Adam noted, testing the opening to see if his broad shoulders would fit through the gap without snagging.

"Come on, Mr. Football, get in there," Georgia encouraged, placing one small, booted foot on his backside and pushing.

"Hey!" he shouted, losing his footing, tumbling forward into the dirt.

Georgia doubled over with laughter. "Hope you never did that on the field, big guy."

He stood up, brushing dust and grass from his knees. "Real nice, Georgia. You're a riot."

"And don't you forget it," she replied sweetly, climbing through to join him on the other side of the fence. "Come on, you slowpokes. Daylight's wasting."

One by one, they crossed through the hole, standing in a line within the outskirts of the hospital's campus.

"Where do we go from here?" Valerie asked, turning slowly from side to side to get a better view.

Gregory pulled a sheet of paper from his pocket, consulting what appeared to Jackson to be an old map. "You're just full of tricks," he told him, eyeing the antique drawing of building after building.

"I like to be prepared," Gregory responded. "It's the former Boy Scout in me, I suppose. We head north to the main building. I'll be able to get a better set of bearings there. Follow me."

They fell into step behind him, the men leading and the three women bringing up the rear. There was little to see near the plant but that quickly changed the farther away they got. More and more structures appeared on the horizon.

A grouping of cottages sat before them, all but indistinguishable from the surrounding greenery, the ivy and other climbing vines practically camouflaging them. "These were staff housing. Many of the employees, with their families, lived here. Rent free, even."

"That's a sweet deal," Adam remarked.

"Yeah, if you can enjoy rubbing elbows with crazy people," Valerie said sourly.

"That's not entirely accurate," Gregory corrected her.

"It was an *insane asylum*, man. The word's right there in the title. Kind of suggests that you're going to run into a few people who would like to wear you like a dress," Valerie countered.

"Well yeah, there were those patients. Goes with the territory. But," he said, as they continued past another row of cottages, "there were plenty of employees who likely had little intimate contact with those patients. Gardeners, cooks, butchers, this place was like its own city, really. The most violent patients, those you suggest were fond of human dresses, were locked in separate wards and didn't have the access most other patients did. And then you had all the industry."

"What industry?" Georgia asked as she stepped around a pricker bush in her path.

"A shoe factory, a wood shop, a machine shop, a farm, and greenhouses, to name a few," Gregory answered.

"And the patients worked in them?" Jackson returned.

"There's no cheaper labor than patients," Gregory pointed out. "Plus, there was none of the talk therapy or medications back then like you have now. This hospital, and others like it, was opened because doctors believed a beautiful setting and occupational therapy would help the mentally ill. The concept ended up not to be scientifically sound, but they spent a lot of money to find out."

"How did you get interested in all this stuff?" inquired Adam, keeping pace with Jay as they continued toward the main building.

There was a pause before Gregory replied to the question. "My grandmother was a patient here in the fifties. In the early part of the decade, back when they were still doing things like electroshock and lobotomies."

Everyone but Gregory stopped moving forward, stunned into silence and stillness. Of all of them, Sarah appeared to be the most shocked.

"You never told me that," she said, almost accusatory in her tone.

"No," he agreed. "It's not something that comes up very often in conversation."

"Why...why was she here?" Valerie asked gently, and began walking forward to catch up to Gregory.

His long strides had taken him almost out of earshot while everyone else absorbed his revelation. They all hurried to make up lost ground. "She was sent here when my father was very young," he began, kicking at small rocks in his path. "She murdered my uncle when he was only a few days old."

"Jesus Christ," Sarah whispered.

Gregory nodded solemnly. "Had it happened now, they would have diagnosed her with post partum psychosis, I imagine. She drowned Clark in the bathtub. My grandfather came home that night to find my father asleep in his bed, and my grandmother sitting in her rocking chair, singing to Clark's lifeless body. She did not understand at all what she'd done."

"That's the saddest and most awful thing I have ever heard," Georgia admitted.

"Me too," Gregory agreed. "So they sent her here. They put her in Ryon Hall, which is still standing. I'm not sure what state it's in now. It was the building where the most violent patients and the criminally insane were housed. My grandmother was not violent on the same level as many of the other patients, but I would guess since she murdered a baby that probably struck quite a bit of fear in the doctors. She was admitted only a few years before they stopped doing lobotomies. The end of that practice came too late for my grandmother. She received a lobotomy shortly after she came here." His voice sounded detached as he relayed the details. It was an ugly story and one he had not spoken aloud to anyone before.

"My grandfather visited her after the procedure. It was the last time he came. She was completely changed afterward, like they all were. She was docile and quiet and would sit and stare off into the distance, drool running down her chin. When she did speak, my grandfather said, it was as if she was in the midst of a dream. He couldn't bear to see her like that and so he never went back. She died here a year later."

"How did she die?" Adam asked, only barely above a whisper.

Sarah shot him a withering look. "That's hardly appropriate to ask."

Gregory shook his head dismissively. "I never met the woman. It's fine. She was murdered. By a hospital attendant."

"This just gets worse by the second," Jackson stated, appalled.

"It really does, doesn't it?" Gregory agreed.

The group continued through the grass and scrub brush for a few minutes in silence. They were almost afraid to ask anything more about the poor woman. Building after building went by as they continued walking. Some of the designs were jarringly different than others. It was painfully obvious which were from the original Victorian gothic plan and which were of the modern, utilitarian age of development. They began to see more of the gothic buildings as they grew closer to the heart of the hospital.

Gregory spoke again to give them the remaining details of the story because now that he had started to talk about it, he seemed to be unable to stop. "The attendants had taken her from her room to try her out with hydrotherapy."

"Which is what, exactly?" Adam interrupted to ask.

"It was a form of treatment, and I use that word loosely, where you lived in a bathtub."

"You lived in a bathtub," Jackson repeated.

"Yes. Sometimes for up to a month. The idea was that water contained healing properties. In retrospect, it seems crazier than many of the patients must have been. Anyway, they were taking her to the hydrotherapy room and when she saw the bathtubs in there…well, I would imagine her broken brain had a flash of memory of what she did to Clark and she freaked out, as I heard it. She was trying to get away and she started to attack the attendants in her struggle. She bit one of them pretty hard and the attendant retaliated. The hospital tried to tell my grandfather that her heart gave out but from what he saw of her body before her funeral, it's far more likely they beat her to death."

"That's a hell of a family history," Jackson murmured sympathetically.

Gregory smiled wanly at him. "Yes. After I found out about my grandmother, I became preoccupied with this place. I'm happy it's closed. It brought a lot of misery to a lot of people over many years. I suppose I wanted to see it to get a sense of her and what her life was like here."

"And you brought us along for the ride," Jackson commented, a wry note to his voice.

"Well, yes," Gregory answered. "What fun would it be to do this alone? I will admit the way I suggested it was rather ham-handed. And now we've arrived at our destination." He gestured toward a particularly decrepit and enormous building ahead of them.

Enormous was not the proper word. The building was a behemoth before them; built of brick, as they had seen previously in the others. Despite its current sad state, one could see its original grandeur. Four stories high, some arched roofs remained while others had collapsed from rot or fire. There was a central portion and two wings flanking either side of the structure. The brick had crumbled from the top floor to the bottom in areas and the inside of the building was visible. In those sections, each floor collapsed to the one below, all the way to the ground.

"Holy…shit," Jay exclaimed, eyes glued to the building. The group of seven stood rooted to the ground, struck by the sight.

"Where do we go in?" Adam asked, his voice full of awe and curiosity.

"Let's walk the perimeter," Sarah suggested, urging her legs to move forward. "Maybe there's a way in that looks a little less perilous."

"Good idea," Valerie suggested, following Sarah as she walked closer to the building.

"What did they call this one?" Jay asked Gregory as the men began walking behind the women.

"I believe they referred to it just as the main building, or the Kirkbride, after the style of hospital, but I've read it was also called Building 51, after it was titled that on a survey map. I prefer the latter."

They walked around the wing toward the front of the building, noting more of the same from the other buildings with broken windows and graffiti and climbing vines. The ground was littered more here with broken glass and crumbled beer cans and the occasional condom wrapper, which made the women shudder with distaste.

To say the front of the building was imposing would have been an understatement. What appeared similar to a castle turret jutted from the center, with two smaller abutments flanking it at either end. The flanking ends had covered archways leading to the doors. An aging circular drive led from the front of the building. Inside the center of the paved circle must have been beautifully landscaped at one time. There was not even the ghost of the past, just a jungle of tangled weeds and spindly trees where there once was the welcoming area to the facility. Now it appeared like a warning. Adam loosed a low whistle of appreciation as they all absorbed the exterior details.

"It would appear the main door is out of the question," Jackson noted, jerking his chin toward the center of the façade.

The door was heavily padlocked, the lock appearing quite thick as well as new. In addition to the lock, the door had been boarded and fading posters warning that the building had been condemned were plastered in several places. They stood clustered nearer to the archway on the right side of Building 51.

"This one might be doable," Sarah suggested, pointing to the much older looking padlock on the door nearest them.

"Should be a piece of cake," Gregory announced, rummaging once again into his pack for the bolt cutters.

Jackson felt a sense of unease. "You sure you want to do this?" he asked hesitantly.

"Cold feet?" Jay asked, grinning.

"No," Jackson insisted. "I just get a little squirrelly about inhaling asbestos and falling through floorboards. I'm complicated that way."

"So long as we all keep our wits about us, we should be fine," Gregory assured him. "But you're certainly welcome to wait for us out here if you're concerned." With that, he marched up to the door and, with a satisfying chink of metal, made quick work of destroying the lock on the door. He looked up from the door to smile at Jackson. "Though, if security does patrol the grounds, you'll stick out like a sore thumb out here." He pulled the rotting door open as it screeched, protesting each inch of movement. A dank breeze drifted out of the darkened interior, wafting over each of them in turn.

"Oh, that's just plain awful," Georgia complained.

"That's going to be stuck in my nose forever," Valerie agreed, gagging a little.

Adam rolled his eyes theatrically. "Well, you'd better get used to it if you're coming inside. The last thing these floors need is a fine sheen of lady vomit." Both women mock-punched him on the arm in response.

"Ladies and gentlemen, Building 51 awaits," Gregory proclaimed, bowing slightly at the waist, gesturing one hand toward the open door. "Let us explore."

Adam entered first, followed by Valerie, Georgia and Jay. Sarah was next, curtsying at Gregory as she passed. Gregory smiled again at Jackson, waving him on.

Jackson took a last, uncertain look at the exterior. "God damn it," he muttered, and walked toward the gaping black doorway, following Gregory.

CHAPTER FIVE

Their footfalls on the filthy marble entry echoed hollowly off the walls of what must have once been a tastefully appointed area. Now it was in shambles, broken furniture strewn about, paper littering the floor, and paint peeling off the walls in ribbons. Despite the afternoon hour and sunny weather outside, inside was mainly in shadow. Only a few scant beams of light found their way through the windows to illuminate the gloom. The ceiling here was intact, unlike many of the other wings. The terrible smell they had experienced outside was more potent.

The reception area was small, possibly for visiting doctors or tradesmen. Ahead was a short hallway, which Jay and Adam began to head toward. The others followed. All were silent as they pushed farther into the hospital. The hallway ended in the larger reception area which was far brighter than where they had entered.

"You could fit my apartment in this room," Jackson said in a hushed tone. Sarah nodded, coming to stand beside him. The area was large and open, though full of detritus as the other had been. A few of the windows were intact but the majority was broken. Some still held jagged pieces of glass, resembling large teeth in their casements. It gave them a sinister feeling, as if those windows were just waiting for something to attempt to pass through so they could give a nasty bite.

Movement in the silent structure had startled birds taking up residence. Beating wings blew past Valerie's head with a rush of air.

"Damn!" she cried, covering her head with her arms in a protective gesture. "What the hell was that?"

"Just a crow," Adam assured her, jerking to look behind his back to see if there was any more waiting to take flight. He sighed with relief when he didn't spot any more or hear any further movement.

"Quite a welcome," Georgia said, undaunted, and started toward the rear of the reception area, where an open doorway led farther into the building.

"Did you pee a little?" Jay asked Valerie, laughing.

"No, smartass," Valerie retorted, still unnerved. "I'd like to have seen how calm you'd have been it had been you."

"Luckily enough, it chose you," he answered, slinging an arm over her shoulder amiably and led her toward the doorway Georgia had passed through.

Beyond the open door, the interior appeared more modern. Vandals had been unable to completely destroy the large administration desk, which was securely bolted to the floor, but not for lack of trying. What they could not destroy, they painted, and it was covered in countless unintelligible words in flaking spray paint. To the left and right were empty doorways leading to what had once been doctor's offices and visitation rooms.

"I imagine these weren't used much," Sarah mused, pointing to one of the visitation rooms, which still held the placard stating its purpose above the doorframe.

"More than likely not," Gregory agreed, poking his head inside. It held an overturned vinyl sofa, three beer bottles placed on the floor, and a metal bucket. "Once you were here, this was pretty much your world. Families wanted their embarrassments locked away from the rest of the world. Visits would have just been a reminder of the shame of having a crazy relative."

Georgia strolled ahead of Gregory, peeking into the rooms as she passed them. An office, a coat closet, and what must have been a break room. She stopped suddenly, standing in the middle of the hallway, staring into the last room before a doorway they assumed led on to the patient wards.

"What's that, Georgia? Another closet or an office?" Sarah asked, walking toward her friend.

"I…I don't know," Georgia answered, uncertain. She still did not move or even turn her head.

This piqued the interest of the others, who stopped peering around the offices and moved toward Georgia. They crowded next to her small frame to get a glimpse into the room.

It was smaller than the offices but bigger than the coat closets. There was one window at the far wall, allowing for enough light so they could distinguish the contents of the room. Despite the adequate lighting, what they saw made little sense.

From floor to ceiling against all three walls were white, wooden shelves. Most, if not all, of the shelves were still holding the same contents they had stored for countless years. Some appeared newer than others but most were old and battered. Several had fallen onto the floor, but most remained in their original locations. No more than three had spilled their contents onto the floor.

"The door was closed," Georgia told them quietly. "It didn't want to open, but then it just gave." Dust motes danced in the light shaft, moving on the currents from the opening door. The air in the room smelled mustier than the other rooms, as if it had been closed up even longer. "What are those doing here? What would they still be doing here?"

Upon all of the shelves and floor were stacks of countless suitcases.

CHAPTER SIX

"That might be the creepiest shit I've ever seen," Valerie observed, trying to suppress a chill that ran up her spine.

Dust covered everything inside of the small room but Georgia could still make out the tags on some of the luggage, displaying what surely had been the surnames of former patients. She was unable to drag her gaze away from the room's contents, attempting to make some sort of sense of why they remained long after the hospital's closure. She felt Adam's hands around her shoulders, gently pulling her back from the doorway.

"Why don't we head into the wards now?" he suggested, looking at everyone else for support. Georgia reluctantly backed away, though she kept looking until her feet had carried her too far to see into the gloom any longer.

"Excellent plan," Jackson agreed, stepping toward the doorway ahead of them. It led into a short corridor to the large patient wing to the right of the building. Access to the other wing had to have been off the other archway entrance into the building.

The corridor had once been encased in glass, affording a view to the grounds in any weather. It would have been especially peaceful in winter, those passing through taking in the peaceful sight of the trees and hills covered in a blanket of white. Now, the mullioned windows were but empty frames except for the roof, which contained a smattering of unbroken panes. The broken tiles on the floor were covered by dull green moss, making for a slippery trek to the other, larger building. The wings were separate structures from the main administration building but with the connecting corridors, they combined to make what appeared to be a mammoth structure. There were other buildings on the campus which were larger but their more modern design was less imposing by comparison. The grandeur of the gothic buildings was spoiled by neglect, an affront to their former pride. A modern abandoned building was more commonplace and less likely to elicit emotion.

Adam kept close to Georgia as they passed through the corridor, tailing the rest of the group. She was still unsettled by the suitcases and Adam could sense her anxiety. He was paying more attention to Georgia than to his footing and felt his boot slipping on the moss beneath his foot. He pinwheeled his arms in an effort to regain his balance. One of his hands grasped onto one of the window casements where the glass had been broken out. A jagged piece was still stuck into the frame. As he closed his hand around the sharp edge, he let out a yowl of pain as the glass bit into his flesh.

"Son of a bitch!" he cried, immediately releasing his grip on the metal and fell backward, sliding on the moss and bringing him to a stop at Sarah's feet.

Everyone stopped moving forward and rushed to Adam's side.

"You all right, man?" Jay asked, kneeling beside his friend, concern evident on his face.

The prone figure groaned, clutching his injured hand to his chest. "Nope," Adam muttered, "though I don't know which part of me hurts the most right now. It's a tossup between my knee, my back and this fucking hand."

"Let me see it," Gregory demanded, pushing his way through the others to bend closer to Adam.

"Help me sit up first," Adam requested, stretching out his other hand toward Jackson, who took it and yanked Adam to a sitting position. "Shit," he grumbled. "Those tiles are hard as hell."

Gregory reached for Adam's left hand, which was bleeding profusely from a gash on the palm. The cut was ugly and deep, blood flowing freely from the wound and down his arm.

"Sarah, give me your bottle of water." Gregory's tone was no-nonsense, extending his hand for the water as he asked for it. Sarah complied, thrusting the bottle at Gregory. He took it, unscrewed the cap, and poured the contents over Adam's palm, watching for any signs of glass still embedded within his skin. Seeing none, he handed the bottle back to Sarah and removed his backpack, taking out the first aid kit.

"That came in handy," Valerie remarked nervously, huddling close to Jay as they watched Gregory work.

He was silent and efficient, placing antiseptic ointment on the wound, then covering it with sterile gauze. When finished, he wrapped it with medical tape. "Hold it up," Gregory commanded. "Bend your arm at the elbow and keep your hand level with your heart. You might need some stitches but this should do for now. You're lucky you didn't end up with any shards of glass in your hand. That would have been much worse."

"Well, this feels pretty god damned bad all on its own," Adam said, gritting his teeth. "But thanks. I appreciate it."

"Of course," Gregory replied. "Need a hand up?"

Adam nodded, again reaching out his uninjured hand for assistance. Gregory and Jackson pulled Adam to his feet, not letting go until they were sure he could put weight on the knee he had twisted during his fall. It was tender but he was able to walk. Georgia came to his side immediately, putting an arm around his waist on his right to help prop him up. "Why don't you guys go on ahead?" she suggested. "We're going to take our time until he's feeling a little better. We'll catch up."

"I'm not sure that's a great idea," Gregory disagreed.

Jackson was not thrilled at the prospect either. "We can wait, Adam," he stated. "It's not a big deal."

Adam waved them on. "It's fine, man. Me and the lady will just sit for a bit. You guys go take some cool pictures or something and we'll find you. We have our cell phones if we get lost."

Gregory still appeared unconvinced at the suggestion. "It's probably best if we stick together," he protested, though weaker this time. Daylight was wasting, he knew, and he wanted to see more before it became late and it would impede finding their way back to the fence near the power plant.

"They'll be fine," Sarah assured him, steering him toward the doorway to the ward. "Once Adam's better, they'll find us. C'mon."

He pursed his lips, nonplussed, but allowed Sarah to lead him into the larger building. "Call if you get lost. And keep that hand elevated."

"Yes, sir," Adam retorted, offering a weak salute as the other five set off ahead. They stepped gingerly over the remaining tiles in the corridor until they reached the doorway to the ward, which was devoid of moss. The walls provided enough shelter from nature to keep it from growing within the ward.

"Let's see if we can find someplace you can sit for a while," Georgia suggested, looking to her left and right.

Ahead of them was another desk, which sat in front of what had once been an office. The hallway led off to the left and to the right, presumably to patient rooms. On either side of the desk where the halls began were barred doors, which now hung open, unlocked. Georgia stepped out from under Adam's arm and peered around to the back of the desk. There was an old chair behind the desk which had escaped the attention of previous vandals. It was filthy and the vinyl was torn, but it would do.

"Come on, take a seat," she told him, pointing behind the desk. "You can pretend to be the receptionist for a while."

Adam limped to the chair, sinking down onto the seat gratefully. "Only if you're going to pretend to be a patient," he laughed weakly.

"I'm sure there must be something about me that would have landed me in a place like this years ago," she agreed. "What do you think would have gotten me committed?" She waggled her eyebrows suggestively, making Adam laugh.

"Don't do that," he said, trying to suppress his humor. "It makes my hand hurt worse."

Georgia frowned. "Well, that's no fun. All right. I'll be completely boring and we can talk about politics or something else. Maybe the mating habits and life cycle of the fruit fly."

"Ugh. That's no good either," Adam grunted.

"Well, there's just no pleasing you then," Georgia sniffed, crossing her arms in front of her body. "How about you just sit there and try to relax."

"That's a brilliant idea. I'm glad I thought of it."

Georgia rolled her eyes. "Yep, you're a dang genius, Adam. I'm a very lucky woman."

"Be nice. I'm injured."

"I'll do my best. No promises, though." Georgia kissed him briefly on his forehead, smiling.

They were far enough away from where Adam had fallen that neither of them could see the small pools of blood shimmering on the marble tiles, nor could they see when the pools slid between the tiles and absorbed into the ground.

CHAPTER SEVEN

"I still can't believe they never cleaned this place out," Sarah observed with disgust as the now smaller group rounded another corner in the patient wards. "There's such a ridiculous amount of...stuff here. You would think the state or whatever would have shipped it off to other hospitals to save money or something."

Gregory scoffed at the suggestion, an action swiftly met with an irritated glance from his girlfriend. He swallowed the rest of his laugh before speaking. "A private company may have done something like that but not the state. Much like the federal government, there's a horrifying amount of waste. They just left this place to rot. Hospitals were closing all over the country and all over the state so there was little need for all of the furniture and everything else here."

Mollified, Sarah nodded. "It's just so eerie. The whole place."

The corridor they were currently walking was the same as the three they had walked prior. It had been a quarter of an hour since they had left Adam and Georgia behind in the reception area of the wards. Since then, they had seen uniform wards of abandoned patient rooms with thick doors, their small windows lined with wire between the panes. The doors stood open now, appearing as though there had been a site-wide prison break and all the inhabitants had escaped all at once. Metal framed beds still stood in the rooms, waiting for someone to lie upon them once again, on the thin, torn and moldered mattresses where former patients had slept and dreamed. Gregory had suggested they check out the second floor to see if it held anything more interesting, since he was of the opinion vandals would have been more likely to stick to the ground floor. There had been no forceful objection to the idea, and they had cautiously ascended the staircase. At one time, it must have been quite grand with its darkly stained banister and curving stairs which climbed toward the sky. Much like every other item that had once held any kind of beauty, the bloom was off the rose. The paint, a cool, Pacific blue, peeled and flaked onto the stairs, making them slippery. The banisters and finials were pockmarked from falling debris or careless explorers. The air and exposure to the elements had taken their toll on the finish.

While wandering the second floor wards, there had been one detour for safety. It had come upon them with little warning, and

Valerie had almost plunged into a hole in the floor. Jackson had acted quickly and grabbed her hand before she could step into nothingness. She had been careless, looking behind her at the others as they had shared a laugh and she had come close to paying the price.

"Jesus Christ," Valerie choked, standing close to the edge of the floor collapse. Too close, Jackson thought to himself as he pulled her back farther from the decayed wood.

"You're not kidding," Jay agreed. "You almost ate shit on that one, Val."

"It's a good lesson to be more careful around here, that's for sure," Sarah agreed. "We have no idea what's around any corner."

The expanse before them was a massive hole torn into the hallway floor where the floor above had rotted through. Planks of wood from the floor hung down from the floor above and to the floor below. Wiring hung down as well, along with a six foot radiator suspended from the third floor. That sight frightened Jackson more than the hole itself, knowing if that gave way, anyone standing below would not stand a chance.

"So, I say we go down this way instead," Jackson suggested, turning to backtrack and take the hallway in the opposite direction. The longer he spent inside this place the more second thoughts he was having. No matter how much research Gregory had claimed to have done on this place, it clearly had not been enough. There was more danger than any of them had anticipated.

"Hold up a moment," Gregory objected, taking the lens cap off his camera. "I want to get a few shots of this before we move on. There's some great light here."

"Take your photos, Ansel Adams. I'm moving down the hall to get away from any shitty sagging flooring," Jackson informed him, stepping away and pulling Valerie with him. She did not object.

Sarah stood next to Gregory in solidarity, pointing out different angles for his photos. Jackson sighed but kept walking, Valerie and Jay in tow. They moved on to a safer section of hallway, the only difference being a different color paint that marginally remained on the walls, a bilious pink instead of the light blue.

Jackson walked farther down the hallway, noting an empty doorway leading to a room larger than the patient rooms they had been passing. This looked to have been some sort of day room, large windows in the far wall with the recognizable remnants of casual furniture strewn about. There were broken coffee tables and more comfortable chairs than the usual industrial chairs they had seen on the first floor. The floor in front of the windows was similar to the hallway they had just viewed as it was caved in, more wooden planks jutting vertically from the sinister maw of the hole.

"Well, we aren't going in here," he informed the others, backing out of the doorway. To the right of the entry was a small door set about three feet off the ground with a rusty metal latch. Curious, Jackson grabbed it, mindful of any sharp edges, and cracked it open. It only protested slightly under the pressure and then swung wide. A foul smelling breeze wafted out, hitting him in the face. He grimaced, but was undeterred in peering inside.

A fraying rope hung within, on a pulley system. Jackson stuck his head in farther; the possibility of bats only occurring to him after his head was fully ensconced in the opening. He looked down and could discern the outline of a metal or wooden tray on the floor below him. A dumb waiter, probably out of use for decades. Most surprising was that the rope was still intact. Jackson thought again about bats, and his hatred of them, and ducked his head back out again. Moving too quickly, he cracked the back of his skull on the top of the frame, eliciting a sharp curse.

He put his hand to the back of his head to check for blood. His fingers came away dry. He blew out a grateful breath and pointed to the door with his other hand. "Don't bother looking in there," he told Valerie and Jay. "Dumb waiter."

"Thanks for solving that mystery," Valerie laughed, a trifle high pitched. Both men could tell she was still rattled about her close call, and neither could blame her for her nerves. They were unsettled as well.

They were rejoined by Sarah and Gregory then as they came down the hallway to them, chatting about other photographs Gregory wanted to take on the site. Sarah spotted the hole in the wall next to Jackson. "Ooh, what's that?" she asked, headed toward him.

"Dumb waiter," Jay and Jackson answered in unison. "Don't bother."

"Bats?" Sarah asked Jackson.

"I didn't see any but that doesn't mean they aren't there," he replied, feeling his stomach roll at the thought. He hated those little winged rat bastards, and Sarah knew it. She had spent almost an entire evening once doubled over in a laughing fit when a bat had gotten into his apartment. He had spent an hour trying to catch it, running from one end of the apartment to the other in his boxer shorts, armed with a tennis racket and a pillowcase. In the end, Sarah had managed to shoo it near a window, which she opened deftly and knocked the vermin out, slamming it back shut before it could re-enter. She had demanded he hail her as a ninja and had gotten a stitch in her side from laughing at him.

"Also, don't go in that room either," he told her and Gregory, pointing a thumb behind him. "The floor is caved in there as well."

"That sounds to me like it might be time to move on to another building," Gregory said. "The newer buildings are likely safer than this one."

"Just because they're newer? They've been empty just as long," Jay protested.

"Many of the older ones have been empty longer than the newer ones but these buildings; the originals were built with wood, which they knew in retrospect to be a terrible idea. It's the wood that's the main cause of these collapses. The newer buildings have steel in their frames, along with concrete. They're sturdier but that doesn't mean they aren't dangerous in their own ways," Gregory responded. "There's much more to see. I think we've exhausted this one's interesting qualities."

Jackson shrugged, "Lead the way, then." Jay and Valerie nodded, following as Gregory headed toward the staircase to go back down to the first floor.

"What about Georgia and Adam?" Valerie asked. "Shouldn't we tell them? They'll be pissed if they come here and can't find us."

"Good point," Jackson nodded. "I'll send Adam a text." He stopped for a moment, pulling out his phone. He fired off a quick message. *Left bldg. Going 2 another. Txt later.* He hit send and immediately placed the phone back in his pocket without a second glance.

CHAPTER EIGHT

It wasn't often the hospital had visitors. Every few months, a group of the curious would sneak inside and explore the halls and rooms within the buildings. They rarely stayed long. The grounds were dangerous, most knew that before they ever breached the fencing, but the hospital itself posed its own threat.

There were times the visitors would run out in a panic, as if they had seen or heard something they were unable to explain. Most times, they wandered in and wandered out inside of a few hours after taking a souvenir of old records found in an office or a piece of wood or brick. There were those who had decorated the walls both inside and out with spray paint or broke windows, feeling young and impetuous as they did so.

This visit was different than the others. Their intent to observe and take photographs was outside the usual behaviors of its visitors. This group had come with respectful intentions. They had disturbed nothing, shown no disrespect or malice, only wonder and curiosity.

When they arrived, the hospital had been dormant. The only movement within the decaying walls was the flutter of birds' wings as they sought new perches or the wind through the broken windows.

But now blood had been spilled.

Doors which had been locked securely now creaked open, welcoming entry. All the dangers which previously were only potential hazards now waited for unsuspecting feet to tread over them. Tattered remnants of curtains fluttered on their rods to an invisible breeze. Shadows roamed empty halls. The hospital was waking up.

The suitcases remaining in the closet Georgia had found were there for a special reason.

Their owners had never left.

CHAPTER NINE

"How's your hand?" Georgia inquired, stepping away from the desk against which she had been leaning and walking across the room to peer out one of the screened windows to the courtyard. The shadows were lengthening outside as the hour grew later.

"The bleeding seems to have stopped but it's throbbing like a son of a bitch," Adam confessed. "All things considered, I got lucky." He spun himself around in a circle on the ancient desk chair, holding his injured hand out in front of him.

"Feel up to looking around a bit more before we go after everyone else?"

Adam considered the proposition for a moment before answering. "Why not? At least we can look at things without getting a history lesson about everything that's ever happened here."

"Aw, c'mon, that's not so bad," Georgia scolded him. "I think it's interesting. And clearly he's done his homework. Better than walking in here blind and having no idea what went down or where anything was."

He shrugged instead of answered. "Where do you want to look first?"

Georgia tapped a black lacquered nail against her chin in thought. "Let's head upstairs and see what the rooms are like up there."

"Lead on, then," Adam answered, gesturing her for her to precede him down the hall to the stairwell.

The pair climbed the staircase, noting the impossibility of moving silently. There was a dense coating of paint chips and crumbling plaster underfoot, not to mention the cans, bottles, papers and broken glass that littered every hallway. At the top of the stairs, Georgia decided to go to the right instead of the left, unknowingly avoiding the collapsed floor.

They passed through wired doors, locks long ago rusted out of usefulness, unable to provide the security they had been installed to enforce. Now their only threat was of tetanus if an unwitting passerby scraped a hand on the bars. Beyond the doors lay a long hallway with a line of opened patient room doors on both sides. Each door held a number and small window with metal wire between the panes. Aged fluorescent lighting fixtures hung at drunken angles from the ceiling, teetering on wiring rapidly losing its confidence. Bulbs from failed fixtures had left shattered remains and fine powder along the floor. Random images and nonsensical phrases had been scrawled along the walls between the doorframes. The light was dim, as the ward sat in the shadow of a much larger building across the courtyard. The air was cool but redolent with the scent of decay and disuse.

"Can you imagine living in here?" Adam asked, turning his head to look at Georgia.

"No, not even for a minute," she replied, hugging her arms to her chest, cupping her elbows in her palms.

"Me either," Adam agreed, nodding. He stepped toward her, his much taller frame molding to hold her against him. He rubbed her back to reassure her. The set of her mouth and the darting of her eyes were telltale signs of her discomfort. She was intrigued and concerned at the same time. He bent to kiss the top of her hair then began ambling down the hallway, glancing in each room as he passed.

After a moment, Georgia began to do the same, though at a much slower pace. Adam often joked that it took her twice as long to cover the same distance as he did since her legs were half the length. In this case, she was more focused upon the details of each room than attempting to rush through searching the second floor.

In the second room she passed, she saw an upended bed frame against the wall, the mattress lying forlornly atop the tile floor. Its ticking was sticking out at odd angles, as if someone had slashed it with a knife. It was possible that someone had, she realized. Next to the mattress was a salvaged garbage pail, several old plastic shopping bags and granola bar wrappers. She realized she was looking at the leftovers from squatters, though probably not long term tenants of the building, given the lack of trash build up. With all the rooms within the structure, squatters could stay in a different room every night for months, at least the ones which were still safe enough to walk through.

Georgia walked inside the room, glancing around. There was a small closet along the same wall as the bed frame. The door had been torn off and was nowhere to be seen. Garbage was piled twelve inches high within the closet, mainly comprised of rumpled fabric which appeared soiled and torn. Wild horses could not have gotten Georgia to touch any of it. The wall to the right was bare apart from more graffiti. This message was legible, unlike most of the other questionable art she had seen since they had arrived.

Scrawled in swooping black letters was the word "Run".

"Oh, that's not creepy at all," she muttered, kicking at a grocery store bag near her foot then backing out of the room into the hallway.

She glanced further down. Adam had progressed almost to the end of the passage, near another doorway at the opposite end. He was standing in the entrance of a patient room, his broad frame and height almost filling the empty space, leaning in for a closer look at the contents. Probably more stupid graffiti, Georgia thought to herself.

Adam had made his way through the rooms far quicker than Georgia not just because of a longer stride. His interest was piqued far less than Georgia's and each room appeared much the same to him – ruined, decaying and full of garbage. He had already injured himself once on broken glass; he had little desire to follow up with cutting himself on rusting metal. The room before him had no furniture left, aside from one lonely chair in the center. It had a metal tube frame; the red vinyl cushion and back-rest were torn, yellow foam exposed at the seams. Everything else had been removed. The rear of the room was in shadow. Adam was unsure if his eyes had not adjusted properly, but he could not tell if there was anything in that corner. Squinting, he could almost make out the outline of a shape but was unable to discern precisely what it was. It almost appeared human. Toward the top of the shadow, he thought he could make out the curve of shoulders. He strode further into the room, exiting the doorway.

A brief scuttling noise sounded behind Georgia, and she rotated quickly to find the source. When she took in the room again, nothing appeared out of place. All the garbage and detritus looked to be exactly as it had been seconds ago when she had walked out. A rat perhaps? A mouse in the closet? Regardless, there was nothing inside.

She walked back through to the hallway, looking again for Adam. Georgia saw his foot as he disappeared completely into the room. The door slammed shut behind him.

"Adam!" she cried, immediately running toward the door.

CHAPTER TEN

Adam continued forward, his movements almost dream-like. He barely heard the door close. He was deaf to Georgia's screams of concern from the hallway. He merely moved on toward the shadow in the corner, reaching out his injured arm as if to brush away the darkness like loathsome cobwebs.

As his fingers permeated the darkness, it seemed to dissolve around him. The light in the room changed, growing brighter. Surprised, he looked around once again and was unsettled to see that it was different...somehow. Had the shadows made it appear dimmer when he first entered? The paint on the walls was no longer peeling, it looked fresh and unblemished. The light fixtures were unbroken and glowing softly.

There was still no furniture in the room aside from the lone chair, though it was altered from his original impression. It was as if the chair had just been placed inside the room. The vinyl appeared brand new, the metal gleaming.

Movement from the rear corner of the room drew his attention once again. Where there had been but a shadow, there was now the figure of a man standing there, facing the wall. The figure was tall, easily six feet, but slight in build. He had long, scraggly brown hair which fell past his shoulders in knots and snarls. One arm hung against his body, which was clad in a powder blue hospital johnny. The snaps at the back were done up improperly, making the material hang askew, filthy boxer shorts peeking out at the bottom.

Bewildered, Adam glanced around the room again, unsure if he was imagining this. Had he pivoted all the way, he would have seen Georgia's face at the window, her small fist banging against the glass in a vain attempt to gain his attention. But he didn't, and instead moved forward toward the man in the corner.

Still the man stood, his body twitching every few moments. His hanging left arm would pull up toward his chest in a spasm then drop down to his waist once again. His right arm was pulled up in front of his chest and Adam was unable to see it.

Was it possible an old patient had experienced a breakdown and come back here because it was familiar? Unlikely as it may seem, Adam didn't believe it was out of the realm of possibility. Certainly stranger things must have happened to people who had lived here.

"Excuse me," he stammered, unsure of what to say and feeling stupid as he spoke. He took another hesitant step toward the man. "Are you lost? Can I help you?"

"No...no help," the man replied, sounding more like moaning than words. Adam stopped moving, feeling frozen as the other man began to turn toward him from the corner.

As the man pivoted, Adam could see knobby knees on the naked legs. The front of the johnny was as cockeyed and dirty as the back. There were streaks of what Adam first believed was dirt or mud down the front, thin trails leading down from the neckline. He glanced up quickly to the face, which was neither young nor old. It was a wasted face, a sad face. It was gaunt, cheeks covered in graying beard stubble. He had a hooked nose and thin lips, which moved soundlessly as he attempted to speak further.

Adam noticed the eyes, which were terrified and angry. And something else. Something else about the eyes. He was unable to discern the detail at first, the sum of the parts he'd been observing unable to come together to a whole.

And then, Adam saw it.

He was bleeding from the inner corner of one eye, nearest the bridge of the nose. A rivulet of blood had coursed its way down the man's face before drying there, looking like an angry welt. The blood trail continued down his face to the gown he wore. It was not dirt, as Adam had initially thought. It was blood, all blood.

Adam's eyes were drawn to the man's hands, which he had been previously hiding from view. He was gripping what appeared to be a spike in one hand and a hammer in the other.

Panicked, Adam looked the man in the eye. The terror he had believed he saw in those eyes earlier was gone, replaced with an eager excitement.

"No help, no help, no help," the man repeated, moving toward Adam with surprising speed.

The man in the gown was on Adam before he ever had a chance to react. The man knocked Adam backward, falling onto the chair in the center of the room. The patient, or whatever he was, straddled him, long legs pinning Adam's on either side. He was strong, far stronger than Adam anticipated as he frantically struggled to free himself.

Words had been replaced with a high, keening wail from the lips of the patient. He reached his left hand to the back of Adam's head, gripping a fistful of hair and yanking his head back toward the floor. The man moved one of his legs, pinning Adam beneath a bony kneecap upon his chest.

The spike was cold as it was inserted, almost gently, into the corner of Adam's eye socket, sliding easily through the soft meat. It held in place, standing upright. Adam's eyes rolled, attempting to see around the obstruction.

Adam screamed in horror as felt his bladder release, warmth he barely noticed soaking his jeans. The light reflected off the metal hammer as the man raised it high in the air, preparing to strike.

CHAPTER ELEVEN

Georgia banged relentlessly on the glass, not understanding why Adam could not seem to hear her or why he didn't acknowledge her shouting outside of the room. She knew these rooms weren't soundproof, so why was he ignoring her? Why had he closed the door?

"This isn't fucking funny, Adam!" she shouted, slamming her small palms repeatedly into the solid door. "Adam! Answer me!"

Still no response. From the small window in the door, she could see him standing in the center of the room, head cocked and looking at the rear corner. The light was dim, but she could make out enough to see he was merely standing.

"What the fuck are you doing?" Her throat burned from her screams.

Something happened then. Adam flew backward, landing upon the old chair which sat in the room.

"Adam!" she cried again with renewed vigor, clenching her hand into a fist and banging it against the door.

Adam's head craned back, touching the rear of the headrest, his eyes staring upward. Georgia heard him screaming then, heard the abject terror in his voice as he stared up at nothing, as if he was trapped in the chair. Time froze for a moment for Georgia. She covered her mouth with her hand, trying to make sense of the scene before her.

The metal winked at her, lodged somehow in Adam's eye. His head hung limply back from the chair, blood running from his eye down his forehead, dripping onto the floor. His eyes rolled in their sockets, finally fixing on one location. Georgia. He finally saw her, though far too late. Adam's weight shifted, changing his center of gravity and the chair fell backward.

As he died, his last view was of Georgia's face, streaked with tears and mascara, as she screamed his name over and over again on the other side of the door separating them.

Jennifer L. Place   54

Adam's attacker was nowhere to be seen, having dissolved back into the shadows which had birthed him.

CHAPTER TWELVE

Gregory, Sarah, Jay, Valerie and Jackson stood in the remains of the courtyard after picking their way out of Building 51 and were arguing over where to venture next.

"It's just going to be more of the same of what's in there," Valerie protested, sounding bored, and jabbing a thumb toward the building they just exited.

"Yes and no," Gregory countered. "Ryon Hall was for the violent and unpredictable patients. This building was a catch-all."

"So then the walls will be padded," Jay remarked, sounding exasperated.

Gregory attempted to keep his temper. This was his idea, his plan. The rest of them were just along for the ride. Sarah had insisted they invite her friends along, and he had objected at the suggestion. This was only further proving him right that the two of them should have come on their own. Adam was injured and he and Georgia were separated from the group, and now two more were threatening to splinter.

Sarah jumped into the fray, trying to keep the peace. She knew what Gregory was thinking and that was annoying her more than the disagreement. "How about a compromise?" she suggested, trying to settle them down.

"What compromise?" Valerie inquired, folding her arms in front of her chest.

"Why don't we go to the morgue..."

"Sarah," Gregory started to say.

She raised a finger at Gregory, prompting him to stop speaking. "We'll go to the morgue first. If it's more your taste than ours, we'll split off again and you can explore to your heart's content."

After a moment, Gregory, Jay and Valerie nodded reluctantly at Sarah's suggestion. Jackson had been watching them bicker for the better part of ten minutes, not really understanding what the point was of any of it. There was still light left in the day and they all had flashlights with them. Why not just split off? He had little interest in visiting the morgue at all. The prospect was unnerving to say the least. He was more apt to go to the other ward building than spend quality time in the morgue. He really wanted to go the hell home but knew that wasn't an option and knew better than to try to find his way out on his own.

"All right then," Gregory murmured, consulting his printed map again. He raised his head and scanned the view before him, glancing at the buildings ahead of them. "The morgue is that way." He gestured off to the left, past another massive decaying building. "It shouldn't be too far past that one there."

"Lead the way," Jackson instructed, waving him on and falling into step. Sarah looked at him gratefully and then turned to keep pace with Gregory. Jackson walked behind the two of them. Jay and Valerie trudged behind him, still sullen about the disagreement despite getting their way in the end.

Flies and bees circled as they walked through tall grass, lighting briefly on their heads and backs as they continued on. They all brushed the grasses and weeds aside impatiently, all wishing they had thought to bring a machete or something similar along to make the trek simpler.

Jackson heard the slap of something hitting flesh followed by Valerie crying out in pain and anger. Jackson turned to see Jay doubled over with laughter and Valerie grasping her elbow with murder in her eyes.

"What the hell?" Jackson asked.

Jay was still laughing, so Valerie answered. "This asshole snapped me in the arm with a sapling," she answered through gritted teeth. "Real nice, Jay. Real goddamn nice."

Jackson smirked. Typical. "Are you all right?" he asked her, biting on his lip to keep from smiling any wider.

Val sighed dramatically. "Yes, I'm fine. But if this chucklehead pulls this shit again I will not be responsible for my behavior."

"Understood," Jackson agreed, nodding. "Onward then?"

She smiled at Jackson and grimaced at Jay. "I'm walking with you. At least you won't try to hurt me."

"Nope, I would never," Jackson answered. Jay recovered himself and began walking again. Sarah and Gregory had stopped a few paces ahead, waiting for them to catch up. Both of them looked annoyed and Jackson found that he didn't care. He assumed Jay and Valerie felt the same way.

They continued on through the grounds, passing what Jackson assumed was another patient ward to their right. It was more modern than the main building, obviously a later addition. Wire screens covered the windows, most of which had the glass broken anyway on the lower floors. There was a screened area that spanned all of the floors. It appeared to be a porch for each floor, where patients could sit and get some fresh air while still being caged like stray animals at a shelter.

It seemed inhumane to Jackson. The entire location seemed to exude desperation and sadness. What sort of life must these people have led over the almost century and a half this hospital had run? Despite the "amenities" it had boasted, what was a typical day like, spent in a locked ward where there was always someone in authority to tell you where to be, what to do, what to eat? Perhaps it was soothing for many of them, who perhaps did not possess the faculties to make those decisions for themselves. Either way, Jackson counted himself lucky to have never experienced anything approaching that type of life.

As they rounded the corner of the building toward the rear, Jackson felt the hair on the back of his neck rise in warning. He looked up at the building, rows of windows rising toward the roof, seven stories above his head. His eyes stopped at a window on the fifth floor, and he froze.

A figure stood in the window. From this distance, Jackson was unable to discern finer details but could see that it was a woman;

long dark hair flowing down around her shoulders. He couldn't see her facial features clearly, only shadows where her eyes and mouth were. For a moment, he thought perhaps his eyes were merely playing tricks on him, that there was a slant of light hitting the glass that merely made it appear someone was there. Apophenia, he believed it was called, when the brain attempted to make sense of random things.

Jackson blew out a deep breath, shaking his head and feeling foolish. They had been in this place a few hours and now he was seeing things. His imagination was getting the better of him. Relieved, he glanced up again to the window, expecting to see it empty like the rest of them.

Except the figure of the woman was still there, staring at him. And then she waved.

"Jay? Jay? Did you see that?" Jackson asked, startled, gesturing toward the window.

"See what, man?" Jay replied.

"Up there. Fifth floor."

Jay stepped next to Jackson, eyes fixated in the direction Jackson was pointing. Jay squinted, standing on tiptoe in a vain effort to get a better view. "Nope, I don't see anything, man. Just more of the same shit we've been looking at. What was it?"

"There was a girl. In the window," Jackson told him. His voice sounded reedy and whining and Jackson hated it.

"Don't yank my chain," Jay scoffed. "Now you're just trying to get me back for whacking Val with that branch."

"What's going on?" Sarah asked, realizing the two men had dropped behind and stopped walking.

"Jackson said he saw a woman up on the fifth floor," Jay replied, skepticism dripping from his voice.

"Unlikely," Gregory chimed in. "We'd have noticed anyone else around here by now."

"Bullshit," Jackson retorted. Sarah and Gregory looked aghast. Undeterred, Jackson continued. "You've said yourself how big this damn place is. How many buildings were there originally? There's no way in hell you would know if there was anyone else here. It's not like there's a goddamn parking lot so people can trespass on a fenced and locked abandoned mental hospital. Just because we didn't come across anyone *so far* does not mean there is no one else here. It merely means we have not seen anyone else."

Gregory strode over to where Jackson and Jay stood in front of the building. He huffed before speaking. "Which window?"

Jackson stabbed a finger toward the window which had held the figure. "That one."

"Well, there's nothing there now."

Sarah and Valerie joined them. They agreed there was nothing there.

Jackson wanted to shout. He wished he had hair to tear out in frustration. "I know there's nothing there now," he growled. "But there *was* someone there before."

"Unlikely," Gregory repeated.

"She fucking waved at me," Jackson protested. "She fucking *waved*. And you think I made that up? Could someone who's known me for more than five minutes please explain to our resident skeptic that I don't routinely hallucinate, do drugs, try to pull pranks on friends, or make up shit that never happened?"

"It's true," Valerie spoke up. "That wouldn't be like Jackson at all. I don't see anything there now but I can't imagine that Jackson imagined it. It's just not like him." Jay nodded as well.

Sarah rolled her eyes. "Well, nothing to be done about it. Either you saw someone else who's doing the same thing we are or the light got in your eyes. Let's move on." She turned on her heel and headed back in the direction they had been going. Gregory walked alongside her, neither of them looking back to see if the others were following.

Valerie looked helplessly at Jackson, shrugging. "I don't know what to tell you," she remarked, placing a hand on his shoulder. "I believe you saw something, but since the rest of us didn't, well, I don't know. Sorry they're being dicks about it, though."

Jackson sighed, slumping. "Thanks," he told her, giving her a smile that didn't reach his eyes. He had been unnerved before but this...this scared him. He began walking again as well, taking long strides to make up lost ground. He continued to tell himself that it had just been a trick of the light on the glass or someone else doing exactly the same thing they were.

Except he didn't believe that. Not at all.

CHAPTER THIRTEEN

Georgia slumped forward, bent in half at her waist, retching violently. Her stomach contents emptied onto the floor, leaving a burning sensation in her already tender throat from screaming. What the hell had just happened? What had been in that room with Adam?

How? How could any of this be happening? She propped herself up with one arm braced against the wall. Still dry heaving, she was unable to move. Her breaths came fast and shallow as she tried to pull herself together. She did not realize she was weeping until she tasted the salt of her tears in her mouth, swirling with the excess saliva from the vomiting.

What she wanted to do was curl up in a ball and cry herself out. What she really wanted to do was to go back in time and never have come here in the first place. Instead, Georgia thought of things she could actually do. First was to find the others and tell them what had happened to Adam. She knew better than to harbor the hope that he would be all right. Adam was dead and she knew it. The how of it she could not explain, could not begin to wrap her head around, because none of it made any sense at all.

There had been no one else in that room with him when he first entered it. But something had to have been in there. Because something in there had killed him. There was no way he had done this to himself, he had made no movements to have stabbed himself in the eye. She had not looked away from him, not even for one second.

When the dry heaves slowed and she was no longer drooling, she stood upright. Still panting, she dug her cell phone out of her pocket, bringing the small screen to life. She could call Sarah or Valerie and find them and tell them everything.

The wallpaper on her phone screen was enough to wrench a sob from her – it was a photo of her and Adam from the week before, sitting curled together atop a large rock from a hike they'd gone on in the mountains.

"Get it together, girl," she chided herself, swiping to her phone book. She found Sarah's number and pressed the call icon with a trembling finger. The dialing screen popped up.

Nothing happened.

Georgia glanced at the top of the phone screen. Where normally there would have been displayed at least two bars of service, there was nothing.

"Fuck!" she shouted, cancelling the call and stuffed the phone back into her pocket. The building had to be blocking her reception. She would have to get outside to attempt the call again.

Her shoes crunched upon the debris on the floor as she turned and ran back toward the stairs she and Adam had ascended to explore the building. She sped down the stairs, grabbing the banister to keep her balance.

When she rounded the final turn, she jumped off the third to last step and picked up her pace. She passed the ward reception desk, barely giving it a second glance. She did think to slow herself a bit while traversing the breezeway, remembering how Adam had slipped on the moss covered tiles.

Adam.

"Damn it, Georgia, not now," she muttered, stepping gingerly around the greenest tiles, moving ever forward. There would be time to mourn Adam; there would be time for tears and for guilt, but that time was not now. Now she needed to get her ass out of this place as fast as possible and find her friends.

The sounds of her ragged breathing and her footfalls were the only things to be heard in the administration building. All was quiet and empty as it had been when they had first entered. The only thing different was that the light and shadows had altered as the day had grown later. The sun was dipping lower in the sky outside. She wondered exactly how long they had been there. It appeared later than it felt.

She violently shoved the door through which they'd entered, coughing and sputtering as she stepped into the fresh air, free of that building's suffocating embrace. Georgia stopped to catch her breath for a moment before taking her phone back out again. She checked the clock. Six. How the hell could it be six already? They hadn't been there that long. They had only been in one building. Well, *she* had only been in one building. It didn't seem possible that so many hours had passed.

Again she dialed Sarah, watching the dial screen come up.

Again, nothing happened.

"Come on, come on," she urged the useless device, shaking it. She closed everything on the phone. Turned it off. Turned it on again.

No signal.

She stabbed her fingers violently against the glass screen, willing the call to go through. Georgia let out a howl of frustration. She wanted to smash her phone into the ground and stamp on it until it shattered, and why not? It amounted to being a four hundred dollar paperweight at the moment.

She was going to have to go looking for them, then. She had no other option. She couldn't just sit here and do nothing. She needed to act. She took out a bottle of water from her backpack and drank half of it before placing it back inside.

Steeling herself, she adjusted the strap of her pack and set off in search of the others.

CHAPTER FOURTEEN

Similar to Building 51, the front door to the morgue was securely locked and boarded, preventing entry. A quick walk to the rear of the building proved more fruitful; the door was held in place with a small padlock which Gregory snapped away with his bolt cutters.

The door was constructed of metal and creaked in protest when it had been freed. The interior was dark thanks to a decided lack of windows in the building. Natural light may have been a distraction given the nature of the structure's purpose. More efficient and constant electrical lighting would have been necessary for the hundreds of autopsies conducted inside over the years.

Before entering, they drew their flashlights and snapped them on, the beams reflecting the dust motes swirling from the disturbance of the air.

"Probably asbestos," Jackson grumbled, pulling his shirt over his mouth, resolving not to breathe through his nose while inside to mitigate his exposure. He noticed the others followed his lead and did the same with their shirts.

Moving forward in tight formation was helpful with lighting the back entrance. "I thought you weren't supposed to cross the streams," Jay joked, his boots crunching on broken glass as they headed farther into the morgue.

"I think that's restricted to proton packs," Sarah corrected him. "Flashlight beams should be fine."

"Oh, right," Jay answered. "I stand corrected. But either way, no one should be thinking about marshmallow men."

The room in which they stood must have been used for shipping and receiving, though what would have been shipped or received apart from corpses, Jackson couldn't imagine. He noted a desk in one corner, an overturned rolling chair behind it, and stacking trays scattered across the floor along with myriad papers. He stooped to pick one up and saw, to his horror, that it was a copy of a death certificate. From 1955. What on earth were these still doing in the building?

"Check this out, guys," he called to the others, shining his light on the form.

Valerie and Jay moved next to him, Sarah and Gregory taking a moment to look around further before stepping beside Jackson. They all peered over his shoulder to get a better view. The form was filled out in longhand, a spidery crawl difficult to decipher before the added difficulty of age, dirt and exposure. Jackson tried to read aloud what he could make out. "Name: James Tanner. Age: 45 years." Jackson paused, straining his eyes to make out the handwriting. "Cause of death: skull fracture." The rest was unreadable but he handed the sheet to Sarah so she and Gregory could get a better look.

All other details were illegible. There were hundreds more upon the floor but none of them really wanted to read them. Gregory showed interest but seemed unsure of being the only one. Instead, he turned and swept his flashlight beam around the room once again. There were broken shelving units and battered filing cabinets, their drawers open to different lengths, looking similar to a row of jagged teeth in a rotting mouth. There were few folders or papers left in the cabinets; it appeared that was where the carpet of papers had originated.

To their right were a few metal gurneys lined against the wall. The metal had long since lost its luster. Now covered in dust and grime, the only shine came when the light hit a spot where fingers had wiped through the filth. Glass-fronted cabinets hung above the gurneys appeared to hold office supplies. Vandals had spared the glass in the doors, having tired themselves out breaking the metal filing cabinets and throwing the records on the floor.

Gregory passed through the rest of the room, reaching a doorway leading to the storage room. Human storage. The room felt smaller than the preceding and, after he considered it a moment, Gregory realized why. The free space in the room was smaller to accommodate for the refrigerated units installed to hold the individual bodies until they were picked up by funeral homes or claimed by the state or loved ones. Perhaps loved ones wasn't the right term in most cases.

On either side of the room were cavities with runners along the bottom of each to accommodate the sliding trays which held the bodies. There were nine slots on each wall. Gregory walked through this room quickly and moved to the next, which was identical; another eighteen chambers to keep the deceased.

"How many people died in here at a time?" Sarah asked, standing behind him. He could hear the disgust in her voice as she asked. Her voice echoed off the tile walls, sounding eerily hollow to his ears.

Gregory cleared his throat before answering. "Well, they did have six thousand patients here at its peak, so really there could have been quite a few at a time. And then you have to figure that they used this building not only for the mental patients but for the tuberculosis patients as well. There's more than likely at least one more of these rooms in this building."

They realized he was correct when they moved through yet another of the same type of room beyond the second. Jay, Valerie and Jackson followed behind, flashlights bouncing as they made an effort to get a look into every corner. Jay seemed particularly captivated by the storage units, standing in front and peering in to see if they contained anything from their former occupants. The doors had all been removed from the slots in each room. Valerie shivered at the thought of being locked alive in one of those coffins. She took Jay by the arm and led him through the last of the storage rooms to catch up with the others.

Beyond the storage was a hallway which led to the front of the building. At the end, it opened into a reception area. There were rooms off each side of the hallway. Most of the placards had been removed from the walls, either taken as souvenirs or broken and crushed underfoot, but one remained. It was labeled Autopsy Suite C.

"That's all you, tough guy," Valerie informed Jay. "I'm not going in there."

"You're afraid of medical equipment now?" he retorted, heading toward one of the suites.

Valerie snorted. "No, dumbass. I just don't need to go in there. Whatever you say is in there, I'll take your word for it." She walked instead down the hallway toward the reception area. Sarah and Gregory followed her down. Only Jackson showed any curiosity about the rooms. He went into the room across the hall from the one Jay was investigating.

"You don't want to take photos of this?" Jackson asked Gregory, surprised. "I figured you would be all over this."

"No, this building is a bit more modern. I prefer the more artistic shots from the older building," the other man replied, sounding only slightly unnerved.

"Right," Jackson agreed, suppressing a smile. Artistic my ass, he thought to himself.

The room contained undisturbed equipment, mainly due to the fact that it was bolted to the floor. A metal table was rooted to the center of the room, large bolts in its feet, securing it to the tiled floor. Jackson could see drains located at several intervals in the floor. Knowing their purpose, to wash the room down and clean away any unmentionable fluids, made his gorge rise in his throat. He moved his light to the edges of the room. There was a rolling cart on its side, along with another broken chair and a cheap industrial desk which was missing its drawers. Any and all medical instruments would have been removed or stolen long ago, so Jackson was unsurprised by their absence.

Despite its austere appearance, the air in the room felt heavy and close. Knowing what had occurred within its walls gave him a bit of a shiver. How many of those who had been rolled into these rooms had perished of natural causes or man-made? How many murders in comparison to infirmity or age? Had any of them been staff or only the patients?

He was creeping himself out, and promptly stepped back into the hallway instead of making his internal disquiet any worse. Jackson walked toward the reception area to join the others, purposely not glancing into any of the other autopsies on his way.

"So there were laboratories upstairs," Sarah remarked as Jackson stepped next to Valerie. A marquee had been spared and the plastic letters fitted into the frame listed out the offices, autopsy suites and the several laboratories which were housed on the second and third floors.

"I'd like to check those out," Jay's voice came from down the hall, where he was still ensconced in one of the autopsy rooms.

"Of course you would," Valerie muttered, looking put out yet unsurprised at his admission.

Jackson glanced at Sarah, who appeared to be out of patience. "I think we're going to move on to Ryon," she announced. "It's starting to get dark and I'd like to see that one before we're relying completely on our flashlights."

"Exactly what I was thinking," Gregory agreed, taking a last glance around the reception area.

"Well, I'm checking out the laboratories," Jay said emphatically, strolling toward them, resolute. "Val, are you going to stay with me or go on with them?"

She sighed. "I'll stay here with you, I guess. Don't want you getting scared in here all by yourself."

"Jackson? How about you?" Jay asked. "Do you want to play mad scientist or are you going to go take artistic photos?"

Gregory bristled at the comment but said nothing.

"I think I'm going to go check out the other building," Jackson answered, after considering a moment. He was unconvinced the laboratories would hold much of interest to him. More than likely, those rooms would be as barren as the autopsies were on the first floor. The quicker they got to what Gregory wanted to do, the quicker they would be done and out of here. And Jackson was quickly reaching his threshold for this adventure.

"Suit yourself," Jay shrugged. "We'll catch up to you in the other building. When you're done in there, we should call Georgia and Adam and see if they're ready to go." He gave a quick wave and started up the staircase off the reception area, Valerie in tow. She gave them all an exasperated glance before disappearing around a turn in the stairs.

"All right then," Gregory said, more to himself than Sarah and Jackson. He turned and began walking toward the back door where they had entered the building. "On to Ryon Hall."

CHAPTER FIFTEEN

The light was fading fast as the trio moved from the morgue and headed toward the building which had exclusively housed the violent and criminally insane patients. Those who posed the most risk both to themselves and others had been kept in that building, none of them enjoying the benefits offered to the more benign residents. There was no occupational therapy, no afternoon tea, and no casual stroll along the grounds or visits to the recreation building. There was merely this building.

Ryon Hall had its own separate infirmary and sitting room. The inmates knew every inch of their cells because that was where they spent the majority of their time. The doors were thick, the walls were padded. Nothing within had sharp edges or anything which could be fashioned into a crude weapon.

Ryon Hall was the one location within the hospital's vast campus where it could be guaranteed one would hear screaming when the lights went out at night and again in the morning. It was the building nurses and attendants hoped not to be assigned to when accepting a position at the hospital. In the early part of the twentieth century, the nurses worked six days a week, twelve hours per day. The daily routine was grueling even in the easier wards with more complacent patients. In Ryon Hall, it felt like punishment. Its halls had housed a woman who had beheaded her two children. There was a former patient who had managed to acquire a piece of metal sharp enough to slit his own throat in his cell, bleeding out before any attempt could have been made to save his life.

As they walked, Jackson fished his flashlight out of his pack, using it to further illuminate their path to the building. Gregory was pushing through the overgrowth at a more rapid pace than he had employed earlier. Jackson could not discern if his gait was due to the late hour or eagerness to see the inside of the structure. Either way, Jackson and Sarah followed. It was too late to back out now.

"Here we are," Gregory announced, stopping a few paces from the front steps of the massive hall. Less gothic and more utilitarian, it still held some of its old character. Wings stretched out to the left and right of the main entrance. Its brick façade failing, it was a sad portrait showcasing how far it had fallen from former grandeur, much like Building 51. The first floor windows were set higher than other patient wards, discouraging escape with their height and the screens upon them. As they had seen before, the front door was barred and locked.

Sarah moved toward the entry staircase, walking along the concrete wall which held the steps. The ground close to the building was devoid of the brush and weeds which could be found throughout the grounds and surrounding the other buildings. For some reason, this one had few things growing near or upon it. Its walls were free of the ivy and other climbing vines they had seen on everything else. She noticed fewer windows broken out and less graffiti.

"I wonder why they seem to have left this one alone," she mused, inspecting the outside.

Gregory grunted. "More than likely because it's farther inside the fence perimeter. They probably didn't want to risk getting caught so far in. Less likely to be able to run back out to civilization if you have a cop or caretaker following you."

Sarah shrugged, unconvinced with his reasoning. "I suppose so. It just seems odd to me that this one is untouched compared to the others."

"So how do you propose we get in here?" Jackson asked, seeing the condemned sign on the door and eyeing the lock. It appeared as new and as sturdy as the one on the main door to Building 51. "The windows are too high for us to reach to get in."

"Here," Sarah said, indicating a basement window near the main entry. The grating had been pried from the casement and the glass had been broken out. Gregory stepped to her side, inspecting the window.

He bent down, fingering the frame. "This had to be recent," he remarked, peering closer. "The break in the metal looks new."

"It works for us that someone else did the heavy lifting," Jackson joked, joining them at the window. "I just hope it's not a far drop down there." His flashlight beam danced down into darkness as they stood before the gaping hole.

Jennifer L. Place   72

"Ladies first," Gregory joked, gesturing for Sarah to lead the way.

"Gee, thanks," Sarah said, dropping down into the grass.

As she crawled toward the broken window, a piercing wail sounded from an upper floor, tearing their attention from entering the building.

"What the fuck was that?" Jackson asked, whipping his head around toward the source of the sound. His eyes frantically scanned the windows, looking for the apparition of the girl he had seen earlier in the window of the other ward. The twilight did not allow for seeing much of anything. Nothing moved near them, nothing else stirred, not even the wind. The sound did not come again.

"Must have been a bird," Gregory answered, unperturbed. "Let's get moving."

"Now or never," Sarah agreed, bracing her hands against the sides of the window, and dropped silently into the void.

CHAPTER SIXTEEN

Valerie was bored. Jay had been poking around in one of the laboratories for the past twenty minutes. She'd had her fill of the room after about five of them. Once she had seen three ancient microscopes and some fractured Petri dishes, she was ready to move on and find the others. Jay was either oblivious to or purposely ignoring her dramatic sighs and eye rolling.

This was the third room they had explored since going to the second floor. The first room they had found was a doctor's office, old wainscoting and chair rail almost entirely ripped from the walls. It had contained a battered wooden desk, the kind frequently employed by stuffy, self-important professionals, and an overstuffed office chair ready to fall off its wheeled base if someone stared at it too hard. Picture hangers still remained embedded in the walls, indicating myriad framed degrees had once hung there. The office had held little interest for Jay, who had strolled casually back out into the hallway after a mere thirty seconds of inspection.

She glanced yet again at Jay's back; muscles moving beneath his shirt as he methodically opened and closed cabinet doors, searching for any memorabilia he could find. Valerie sighed yet again, unable to help herself. As with all the others she had let loose, this one was ignored as well. She blew out a breath, fanning her hair out of her face.

"I'm going back into the doctor's office," she announced unceremoniously. Jay merely grunted in reply, and she stomped out of the room and into the hall, making a sharp right into the office they'd been in before.

During their brief inspection, Valerie had noticed a few filing cabinets in the back corner of the office which appeared to have been undisturbed. Perhaps previous explorers had grown tired of wrecking the things left on the premises by the time they reached this building. Or perhaps they had just never lingered long enough in the office to have noticed them lurking at the opposite end of the room.

There was nothing remarkable about them. There was a trio of standard size, vertical cabinets. The polished wood veneer had long ago dulled from neglect and exposure to the elements. The metal tag indicating the record numbers and the name of the hospital still remained at the top left of each cabinet. Valerie stared at these for a moment, noticing the length of the numeric identifier, wondering how many records the hospital had seen in total in its years of operation.

Gingerly, she tried one of the drawers to see if any records still remained within its confines. It strained against the motion but slid out under her hand with only minimal force. Inside, dozens of file folders hung together; some thin, some straining with papers. Each folder had a tag stating a name and identification number. Valerie chose a folder at random, removing it from the drawer. She stepped across the room and laid it upon the desk, opening it to view the contents, flashlight creating a circle of illuminated text.

Within the folder were the records of a patient – Annette…something. The surname was obscured on the tag and it was difficult to make out the cramped, handwritten notes on the pages. She spotted a date on one of the sheets – 1930. Curious why records this old had not been archived, she began trying to decipher the scrawling hand, picking pages at random.

In 1930, Annette was a patient at the hospital and had evidently been there for quite some time. She was 91 years old in 1930, a surprising age for the time, made more so considering where she resided.

"Patient continues to be unresponsive to treatment. Refused meals for two days. Sent instead to occupational therapy. Unwilling to cooperate, refused to use the loom. When Nurse Avery attempted to return her to her room, patient began screaming uncontrollably. Electroshock therapy prescribed."

A separate set of notes followed.

"This is the third consecutive week of electroshock administered. Patient unchanged. Despite treatment, patient still unwilling to eat of her own free will. Still refuses to attend occupational therapy. Still suffering from dramatic outbursts. Growing violent. Hydrotherapy prescribed."

Valerie was horrified, but continued through the pages. There weren't many more in the file folder. A progress report for the hydrotherapy said little more that she could read other than that Annette had been undergoing therapy for two weeks.

The next page she turned to was the last.

"Patient expired in hydrotherapy tub this morning. Treatment unsuccessful. Note patients of advanced age should not be considered candidates for therapy in future. Death certificate prepared, next of kin notified. Post-autopsy, remains to be transferred to potter's field."

"Christ, that's cold," Valerie muttered, closing the file and replacing it in the cabinet drawer. It seemed wrong to leave it out on the desk. She knew it was a doctor's report, which would certainly have been devoid of both compassion and humanity, but the terse language seemed cruel. That was a person they were treating, someone who, despite their illness, had thoughts and feelings and reading these words, seemed to be thought of more like an object. And what of the next of kin? Valerie was horrified to think of anyone allowing a family member to be buried in a potter's field, that it was too much of a bother to do anything else.

Poor woman, she thought to herself, rubbing her elbows. When this trip had been suggested, she had been eager to go. Similar to the others, she had believed it would be interesting to see what the grounds looked like as they rotted from neglect. There would also be bragging rights to her other friends that they had managed to break in undetected and explore all the buildings. She knew the buildings had contained remnants from when the hospital had been in operation, but there had never been a moment where it had occurred to her that *actual* people had lived and died on these grounds, within these walls.

Men and women had worked here, had spent most of their lives caring for the mentally infirm, for long hours and little pay. Men and women had been patients here, either being dropped off by family who were unable or unwilling to care for them any longer, whether they were ill or merely aged.

Valerie cringed, feeling disrespectful. She felt like an interloper, an intruder. They had all walked into this place that had seen countless tragedy and heartache, and they were treating it like a fun afternoon hike.

She shook herself, resolving to drag Jay out of this building if she had to, go find the others and get the hell out of here.

It was time to go home.

CHAPTER SEVENTEEN

It was fucking dark. Georgia hated the dark. She hated being outside in the dark even more. Inside her bedroom or her apartment she could endure. She knew where everything was in her apartment, every corner of the furniture, every placement of an end table or where she kept her shoes. She could maneuver in her spaces in the absence of light. She didn't like it, but she could deal with it.

This dark she could not.

She moved as quickly as she was able given the impediments of the bushes and grass and pavement. She was unfamiliar with the terrain and the location in general. Ever present in her mind was the potential hazard of stumbling into a gopher hole and breaking an ankle. Gritting her teeth, she resolved to stop panicking at what injuries could befall her and just keep moving forward.

They had to be around here somewhere.

Many thoughts traveled through her mind as she attempted to remain calm and find her friends. She couldn't help Adam now. Adam was still dead in that room back there, alone with the peeling paint and the unsettling, terrible silence.

It was not silent now.

Georgia felt as though the sun setting had somehow brought the grounds to some semblance of life. Each tree, each bush, was terrible in its shadowy outlines. Even with her flashlight trained on the path before her, everything on either side of her was cloaked in darkness and anything could be within it. Monsters, ghosts, other people...anything. The uncertainty and the unknown were as terrifying to her as someone running out in front of her would have been.

She could hear things moving in the dark. What they were, she thought, was better left unconsidered. From the buildings around her she could hear the tinkle of glass breaking, and the scuttle of debris rolling around on dirty floors. Twice she thought she heard someone breathing behind her. Each time she turned around to investigate, she had found the path behind her empty. The fear was starting to loom large within her and her steps quickened, heedless of the potential pitfalls hidden by the long grass.

Foolhardy or not, she began to call out for her friends. "Sarah! Jackson! Where are you guys? I need help!"

Standing still, she listened for her friends for a few minutes.

No response.

At this point, she was unsure of where to turn or where to look. She had been hoping one of them would have heard her call and yelled back, or been out looking for her. Now, she didn't know where to go. Gregory had been the only person with a map of where all the buildings were and what their functions had been. Swiping her flashlight back and forth in front of her as she began moving again, the light licked across a set of concrete steps. She came to a halt, moving the beam up the building.

RECRE TION CENT R, dirty letters in a marquee screamed. The A and E had fallen at some point and now lay upon the steps before Georgia. She took a few tentative steps up the stairs to the doors. They were slightly ajar; whatever lock or bar that had been in place rotted through. She stood at the door, listening. Maybe they had come in here.

Georgia thought she heard voices further inside the building, murmuring to one another in the distance. They were too far away for her to make out the words, but there was certainly more than one voice inside. She heard a woman's tinkling laughter and that spurred her to action.

They had to be in here.

She pulled the door open by its splintering frame and dashed inside.

CHAPTER EIGHTEEN

Sarah's feet hit the ground, sending shockwaves through her ankles and up to her knees. She cursed under her breath, standing still for a moment until the unpleasant sensation lessened. She pulled her flashlight from her pocket and switched it on, sweeping the room ahead of her.

She knew she was in the basement, so seeing pipes running along the walls around her were no surprise. There was a cluster of metal racks off to one corner and a few folded and rusting wheelchairs in another. The floor was concrete and damp in most places, the beam of her light reflecting off the occasional puddle.

"All clear," she called up to Jackson and Gregory. A moment later, a set of feet dangled through the window opening and then dropped to the floor. Gregory stood up, grimacing.

"The landing's a bitch," Sarah remarked, nodding at him.

"It's not far but it's definitely uncomfortable," her boyfriend agreed. He turned on his flashlight, helping to dispel some of the gloom.

Jackson landed behind them, yelping slightly.

"You all right?" Sarah asked, concerned.

"Fuck," he answered. "Twisted my ankle a bit when I landed." He took a tentative step toward them, testing how much weight he could put on it. "I think it'll be all right. Just don't ask me to run anywhere for a while."

"We'll do our best," Gregory replied dourly. "So long as security doesn't show up, you should be fine."

"Not a confidence booster there, Greg," Jackson growled, his already sour mood darkening further from the injury.

Gregory frowned, shadows making his expression sinister. He looked at Sarah. "Did you happen to notice any stairs down here?"

Sarah shook her head. "I didn't notice but then again, I didn't have all that long down here before you got here. Have you noticed any?" To Jackson, she seemed irritated, either for his terse question or lack of concern for Jackson. He couldn't tell which it was and then decided it didn't much matter.

Jackson shined his light toward the far corner of the room on the right. He saw a door in the wall and headed closer to read the plate upon it. He limped slightly but wasn't terribly impeded.

After ten steps or so, he was able to read the door. It led to the boiler room. There certainly wouldn't be an exit to the upper floors from there. That room would be a maze of equipment and he had no desire to take a peek behind the door. He moved farther to his right and could hear Sarah and Gregory following behind him. Pushing cobwebs aside which hung from the ceiling, he kept the same course, sweeping his light ahead of him as Sarah had been doing before.

They had not stopped to consider the size of the basement before they dropped inside. It ran the full length and width of the building above and was a warren of equipment and castoff furniture and other materials. When the building had been abandoned, as with the other ones, most items had been left in their original locations and not moved. For that, Jackson was grateful. Had more items been moved down there, it would have been almost impossible to move.

The empty space in the room did allow him to spot a set of stairs leading up to the main floor. Luckily for them, the door appeared to be slightly ajar.

"This way," Jackson called, urging them forward. "There are stairs over here. And the door is open."

"Fantastic," Gregory said, his voice tinged with excitement. Jackson rolled his eyes, glad the dark hid the action. Gregory overtook the lead, wanting to be the first through the door and into the building proper. Jackson halted his forward momentum, allowing the other man to get ahead of him.

Sarah caught up with Jackson and shrugged. "He's like a kid at Christmas," she remarked, eyeing Gregory skeptically. "He never gets like this."

"Not even when they release a new set of Magic the Gathering cards?" Jackson asked, only half joking.

She smirked. "Not even then. At this point, I'm thinking like I'm his mom. Let him go nuts in here and eventually he'll tire himself out and then we can go home."

Jackson laughed softly. "I thought you were all in on this," he assumed. He noted her stance, how rigid her body was. If she had been having fun before, she wasn't any longer.

"I was," she admitted. "But at this point, I'm over it. It's late, we've been wandering around this shithole for hours, and I just want my pajamas and a cup of tea and some terrible television, you know? Enough's enough."

Jackson agreed wholeheartedly. "Adam and Georgia are probably wondering what the hell we're all doing."

"Like I said, hopefully he'll be done in here shortly and then we can round up the rest of the troops and head back to the house and go home. I'm glad we have the flashlights because I don't know how the hell we'd find our way back out of here without them."

"Are you guys coming up here or what?" Gregory called through the doorway, annoyance coloring his voice.

Sarah sighed. "We're coming right now," she promised. "Jackson was resting his ankle for a minute."

"Oh sure, blame this shit on me," Jackson grumbled, though he was smiling at her.

"What did you think I was going to do, say I didn't care about the stupid ward?"

"Well, since that's the truth, yeah, I guess I did."

"Pfft. You don't even know me at all," she laughed, preceding him up the stairs. "Watch your step before you completely bust your ass. We can't carry you out of here."

"Hilarious," Jackson murmured, but followed nonetheless.

After passing through the doorway to the ground floor, Jackson's initial impression was reminiscent of their prior explorations. Everything was a near perfect carbon copy to the others, down to the peeling paint and drunkenly leaning furniture. The only real change was that the dark made all of it seem exponentially more sinister, as if they were walking through a video game.

Since the hospital in total was not in use any longer, there were no illuminated street lamps outside to lend ambient light through the windows. As the buildings were emptied of patients, the power grids were shut off in those sections to save money. All the old fixtures now stood impotent along the ruined pathways and roads in the complex.

As he had earlier, Jackson pulled the collar of his shirt over his mouth. The flashlight beams illuminated motes of dust and other small particles. Now that he could see what was disturbed by their entry, his concern about asbestos exposure resurfaced.

"You guys should probably cover your mouths and noses," he instructed, pointing toward the beam from Gregory's flashlight. "It looks like it's snowing in here."

"Good idea," Sarah agreed, following Jackson's lead and doing the same. Gregory ignored them both and kept moving forward.

They had entered near staff offices and a break room, which were identical in form to the previous ward they had been in. Gregory led them down a hallway which ended in an unlocked sally port to the patient wards. The sally port consisted of two sets of barred doors, a space in between them for those passing through to wait. The first set of doors had to be secured before the second set opened, ensuring no patients could escape.

"How different could these rooms really be?" Jackson inquired, growing more impatient and anxious by the moment.

Gregory turned back to glance at Jackson, light reflecting off his eyes, making his ordinarily benign face appear almost menacing.

"This is where all the major occurrences went on," he explained. "This was the home of the rapists, the murderers and the psychotic."

"So this was the home of your grandmother," Sarah said, the words slipping out before she could stop them. She saw the shadow of his head nod in response.

"According to the few things I've been able to find out from my family, and from my research, her room was on the second floor. Room 244."

"I'm guessing that's where we're headed," Jackson assumed, groaning internally.

"Precisely," Gregory agreed. He turned his head back and continued to press on toward the sally port.

CHAPTER NINETEEN

Valerie exited the office and headed down the hallway to the lab where she had left Jay. She noted at once both the lack of light coming from any of the rooms off the hall as well as the lack of sound. Perhaps he had run out of cabinets to open and close but she didn't imagine he would be standing in the dark in any of them. She stopped in the doorway to the lab he had been in and realized he must have moved on to a different one.

"Jay?" she called tentatively, her voice wavering. He did not answer. She retreated back to the hallway, shining her light into the adjacent lab. Nothing. Walking down the hall, she shone her light into each, seeing they were all empty.

As she passed the third set of doors, she heard a cabinet door close and heard the unmistakable sound of paint chips crunching underfoot. The sounds had come from the room ahead of her on the left. With relief, she pressed onward and stepped into the room, expecting to find him within.

Except he wasn't in there. No one was.

A gurney lay on its side in the center of the room. A lone filing cabinet stood sentry in a far corner. An examination table had been pushed against the wall to her left, fraying canvas restraints still attached to its sides. Valerie stepped further into the room, now in pursuit of the source of the noises which had led her into that room. Eschewing good sense, she moved farther inside, closer to the rear of the room and the examination table.

"Jay?" she called for the third time, hoping perhaps he was nearby and would hear her and come in. And then she could get the hell out of this creepy old place and go home.

Another crunch of paint chips, this time coming from behind her. Before she could turn around to see who it was, she saw a burst of stars in her eyes as she was struck from behind. Then she saw nothing.

*   *   *

Her head hurt. That was the first thing she was aware of when she swam back into consciousness. Her head hurt from the blow to the back of her skull, and her eyes hurt from the bright lamp above her face.

That stopped her. Light? What light? She had been in a dark room in a building with no electricity. How was it she was squinting her eyes closed against the brightness now? She attempted to bring her hand up to shield her eyes from the illumination and found she was unable. Her arm was firmly pinned down, as was the other. Valerie attempted to move her legs next and had the same result. Brightness be damned, she opened her eyes.

She saw her surroundings and was unable to process them. None of it made any sense at all. Was she still unconscious and this was some sort of dream? Had Jay and the others found her passed out and taken her to the emergency room? That had to be the explanation. That almost made sense. Except why would she be unable to move, unless she had been critically injured when whatever it was had hit her? But that didn't seem likely since she didn't feel particularly bad, apart from a screaming headache that was really no worse than some of the truly heinous hangovers she'd experienced in her early college years.

No, there was an answer here. She just hadn't happened upon it yet.

A shadow passed to her left, stopped. The lamp above prevented her from discerning any facial features.

"Where am I?" she croaked, her throat dry as a desert. "Am I in the emergency room? Am I going to be okay? Where's Jay?"

Soft laughter came from the figure before her. "Relax, my dear. We're here to take care of you. You'll be just fine shortly."

"But where's Jay? Where are my friends? They brought me here; they must be out in the waiting room."

The figure shifted position, pivoting in place to grasp something from behind. "There's no one else here, child," the voice replied in a soothing tone. It was a man's voice, a honeyed tone which came from years of practice speaking in low tones to instill calm. A bedside manner type voice, Valerie noted.

"They *have* to be here somewhere," she insisted urgently. "I couldn't have just gotten here all on my own."

"Oh, I'm sure they're somewhere," he agreed. "But right now we have to concentrate on getting you better. Your friends will all be well taken care of."

Panic and adrenaline flooded Valerie. She attempted again to move, to dash off the examination table but was trapped. Lifting her head from the cold metal with tremendous effort and pain, she saw that her arms and legs were restrained by wide canvas and leather straps. The straps looked familiar to her. She knew she had seen them before. The figure of the man was moving again next to her.

"Don't do that," he instructed, his voice almost a caress over her. "You need to relax. You'll feel better in no time but it would be better if you didn't excite yourself."

"Relax? Are you kidding?" Valerie cried. "Where the hell am I? What the fuck are you doing? Who are you?" Again, she strained at the bands in vain, tendons in her wrists and arms bulging with the effort.

"My name is Dr. Kessler. Everything will be fine. I'm here to get you better," the man insisted.

"I want Jay," she whined, sounding pathetic even to herself. "Please."

"I believe he is on another floor at the moment," he told her after a moment's thoughtful pause. "He's with some of the staff. Don't worry about him." The shadow bent over her then, his face finally coming into view and no longer hidden by the bright glow of the lamp.

The doctor's skin had a pallid, sickly cast to it. His eyes were sunken, cheeks jutting out sharply. His mouth was stretched into a wide grin, exposing two rows of blackened, rotting teeth. As Valerie opened her mouth to scream, Kessler's hands moved with incredible swiftness, placing a gag between her teeth before she was able to utter a sound.

The gag was fastened behind her head with practiced dexterity. He pivoted again, turning back to pick up more necessary equipment for his task. When he turned back to her, he held in his hands what appeared to be a jumble of leather straps whose shape didn't register as anything familiar to Valerie's terrified gaze. Even as he began to untangle the straps and they took on an actual shape, she still did not know what they were.

He placed the straps around her head. She felt two of them pull down along her face then buckled beneath her chin. She began to hyperventilate. The gag obstructed her ability to breathe through her mouth. Her nose was dried out and stuffy from the hours of inhaling particles inside the hospital buildings. Her breathing was rapid and jagged. The slight elevation Valerie could muster with her head allowed her to see the alarming rate at which her chest was rising and falling with every second. Her eyes were wide and unblinking as the smiling visage leaned over her yet again.

Dank breath washed over her face as he spoke. It smelled like grave dirt, rich and fetid with living things feeding on dead ones. "Are you comfortable? It works best if you lay back and are calm." A gnarled hand smoothed her hair off her forehead. His skin felt like a dried corn husk against hers.

She screamed against the gag, a muffled cry no one outside of the room would have been able to hear. Her lips blew out against the obstruction as she tried to draw in more air through her mouth, spittle collecting at the corners in bubbled clusters.

Kessler pursed his lips in disappointment and sighed, expelling more of his humid breath over her face. Valerie could feel vomit rising in the back of her throat and fought to keep it down, knowing it would be disastrous to throw up now.

"I guess we'll just have to make do such as you are," he lamented. "I was hoping for this to be easier. Since you cannot seem to calm down, I fear this will be a bit on the painful side."

Again he reached for something out of her line of sight. Tears began streaming from her eyes and she cried out over and over, all of them lost against the thing in her mouth. Her body bucked uselessly against the restraints which pinned her. She heard the sound of a dial clicking as it was turned in a piece of machinery followed by a low humming. Kessler looked at her pityingly, bringing his hands up to either side of her head with what vaguely resembled bizarre jumper cables. She shook her head from side to side as much as she was able, attempting to keep him from pressing them against her flesh.

"Now, now, I told you, the more you fight the more this is going to hurt," he scolded. She could sense the pulse of electricity emanating from the wands he held alongside her head. "Try to relax. It'll all be over soon and you'll feel so much better. And maybe then you can see Jay again. You want to see Jay, don't you?" Kessler paused, wands suspended scant inches from her temples.

Valerie nodded briskly in response, her eyes wide. "That's very good, my dear. We're going to make you better." The wands moved in closer, and closer still.

They reached her temples. Every muscle in her body tensed in anticipation. The sensation was akin to the feeling she had experienced as a child when her cousin Sean had dared her to lick the contacts of a nine-volt battery. She felt a buzzing throughout her body, starting at her head and moving down to her legs. This she could handle, she thought to herself.

Until the doctor bent over her again. "Not so bad, right?" Kessler breathed the words into her face. "We started out on the low side. Let's see what happens when we move the dial up just a little bit more." His face disappeared from her line of sight again and she heard the hum grow louder before she felt the increased current begin to flow through her yet again. This was pain now, not merely some vague annoyance. Every nerve ending stood at attention.

She saw Kessler's forehead, then face moving again as he bent to speak to her. "Ah, you feel that now," he confirmed, a wry smile curving his dry lips. "This will fix you in no time at all. I'll adjust the frequency again for you."

He hummed to himself as he fidgeted with the machine. "Earlier in my career, a bit before your time, I was the best at this procedure. I had to stop counting the number of patients I helped here. They would come in, horribly broken people, and leave so much better. There was just that one time…that one time that one ungrateful son of a bitch resisted me. Ended my career, too. They were writing papers about the work I'd done, the things I'd accomplished and then that poor bastard broke out of the restraints. The stupid nurse must not have tightened them properly." He sighed, aggravation and disappointment obvious in the sound. "In any event, he broke loose and was able to take me by surprise. The orderlies took care of him, of course, but that was the end for me. As you can see, though, I still do freelance from time to time. I'm more than happy to take on your case. It's been far too long."

The hideous face receded and the click of the dial could be heard again in the room, moving much farther this time until it stopped, or was stopped when it reached the maximum.

Valerie braced herself but was unprepared for the white-hot ripple which enveloped her and did not lessen. She screamed against the gag in her mouth, a scream which likely would have shattered glass yet sounded only like a muffled groan. Valerie knew exquisite pain…and then nothing at all.

CHAPTER TWENTY

The sounds had ceased as soon as Georgia entered the recreation building. She stood for a moment in the center of the entrance, not daring to move a muscle as she listened intently to identify from which direction the voices had come. She was tense, ready to move if she heard anything further. But she did not hear anything apart from the wind as it came through broken windows and sent papers skittering across the tile floor.

"Son of a bitch," she muttered, feeling defeated. They had to be in here. She had heard them, she knew she had. They must have just moved farther into the building and out of earshot. That had to be it. Georgia resolved to sweep the building in search of them. If she didn't encounter them in the next twenty minutes, she would head back to the entrance and then back outside and start calling for them again.

She was so tired. She took a drink of water before setting forth into the building.

As she stepped forward, she noticed this building was far more modern in design than the previous. It was ugly, with none of the old world splendor of the earlier buildings. This was constructed of concrete and masonry, and the interior had the same institutional feel as the exterior. The darkness was easier to take since all of the walls were either the dingy gray of concrete or hospital white. There was the obligatory smattering of graffiti everywhere she went, but she didn't feel as though she was entering a bottomless abyss as she moved onward. There were rooms off the main hallway, some retaining their labeling from when it was open. She passed by the music room, an exercise room, a craft room. There were faded signs high up on the walls with arrows pointing down various hallways, advertising the theater and the pool. She thought perhaps her friends had gone to check out the theater. There would be a certain amount of soundproofing in that room so it could explain the sudden silence.

Georgia turned and began walking in the direction indicated by the signs toward the theater. She swept her light from side to side in an attempt to anticipate where her path would be blocked by debris and abandoned furniture. Several times she had to move to one side of the hallway and squeak past a barricade of tables and folding chairs. It made her grateful for her small stature as she slid against the cool concrete wall past the jumble of junk.

It was a shorter walk than she had anticipated. After only a few minutes she arrived at a set of double doors that were unmistakable as the entrance to the theater room. The door on the left was still standing despite its rotted hinges. Georgia was almost afraid to move either of them, thinking one or both would collapse onto the floor – or onto her. Then she would be pinned and it would be anyone's guess if she would be found. Her friends would not have been able to enter this way. There had to be another way in somewhere. She just had to find it.

Biting her lip, she glanced around her. The hallway split off to the right and left into separate corridors. When she panned to the right, she noticed within an exceptionally bright and nonsensical bit of graffiti a few words which had not been created with spray paint. "Projection Room" had been painted on the wall in block letters with an arrow painted beneath. They were all but obscured by the rainbow tagging. She turned and headed in that direction, hoping the door would be less terrifying.

The projection room was only about fifty feet further down the hallway. As Georgia approached, she noticed the door slowly swinging out toward her. She quickened her pace, thinking perhaps the others were inside. She still didn't hear anything but moved more quickly regardless. She grasped the doorframe with her hand and swung it wide, stepping into the room, flashlight panning the room from left to right.

Nothing. Again.

She growled in frustration. As she moved her light around, she saw a few broken chairs, an equally battered desk, and an old film projector on an ancient stand in one corner. Reels of film littered the floor, having been unspooled and thrown about like streamers at a surprise party. The celluloid crunched under her boots as she moved toward the far end of the room and the opening it gave onto the theater itself.

The window wasn't wide as it was meant for the projector, but given how slight Georgia was, she was able to rest her elbows on the bottom ledge and shine her flashlight down onto the floor for a better view. The room must have once been quite grand, as equally impressive as any theater open to the public for movies and other events. At the far end was a large stage constructed of wood. Moldering black curtains hung listlessly from the rafters, their ends shredded. The floor before it had obviously once been filled with seats, the majority of which had been removed or stolen in the years since its closure. The remainder was jumbled in a pile in one corner to the side. A previous intruder had toilet papered the entire room from front to back. It looked as though a wild party had torn through the room like a tornado, leaving destruction in its wake.

From her perch in the projection room, she had a decent view down onto the room in its entirety. Had she entered through the large doors to the room itself, she would have walked steadily downhill as the floor sloped. The projection room sat well above the floor and she swung her beam of light from one end to the next. She had hoped her friends would have been in the room. They would have immediately noticed the light sweeping from up above.

As she made yet another pass across the room with the light, she spotted movement on the edge of the light on the floor. She quickly jerked the light to the area and as she did so, a pale, moon-like face glanced up at her, grinning broadly.

"Hey!" she yelled in surprise. The face immediately turned back toward the floor, and the person turned and ran back toward the entry doors.

In her haste to follow, Georgia dropped her flashlight, swearing as she heard it clatter to the floor. She frantically searched the filthy floor with her hands, finally feeling the hard plastic beneath her fingertips. She snatched it up and ran out of the room to the hallway, desperate to catch up to whoever had fled the theater.

The delay cost her being right on top of the other person but she could hear their footfalls as they ran down the hallway she'd traversed to get to the theater. She let out a breath and started in the same direction in pursuit. If this was a joke, it wasn't funny. Whatever "friend" was doing this was not going to be her friend anymore after she caught up with them.

Even with going through the furniture barricade yet again, it did not take long to arrive back in the main area of the recreation building. She stopped to get her bearings and to listen for the progress and direction of the person she was chasing. The building was still. Georgia controlled her breathing, forcing herself to slow down so she could concentrate on her hearing.

Georgia would have sworn that she heard laughter coming from the hallway to her left. She cocked her head in that direction, listening intently. She had only heard the sound once, but as there was nothing coming from any other direction in her vicinity, she chose to head that way. It was still under the twenty minutes she had promised herself in the building and she headed off in the direction of the small burst of sound.

As she sped through this part of the building, she noticed it was lighter. She looked up briefly, noting the high ceiling and the expanse of glass panes which ran the perimeter just below, allowing the tepid moonlight to filter in brighten her surroundings. She was happy to be less reliant on the flashlight. She switched it off and gave herself a moment for her eyes to adjust before moving forward.

She moved into what once must have been a common area, round tables lying on their sides, chairs stacked in corners. Concrete planters stood at varying locations, now empty of everything but dirt. Graffiti artists had used the walls inside as a large canvas. Bright murals ran the length of the walls in the area, some of it done by individuals with obvious talent. She stopped again, alone in the center of the common area, listening.

Laughter again, the tinkling notes not close but still audible. Georgia remained still and continued to listen.

"Come and get us!" a woman's voice taunted and was followed by the faint sound of footsteps retreating farther into the building. Georgia moved then, walking as swiftly as she dared. She couldn't tell if it had been Sarah or Valerie but knew it had to be one of them. They were fucking with her now, playing around in the dark. They had no way of knowing that Adam was dead in Building 51, sitting in that solitary chair and growing colder by the minute.

She shook those thoughts off.

Jennifer L. Place   94

Determined, she increased her pace and headed down the hallway. She followed the sounds, which were leading toward the pool, according to the sign on the wall. Georgia began yelling her friend's names in turn as she moved down the hallway. There was no reply, only the sound of her voice echoing off the concrete. One section of the hallway was covered in books, something which took her completely by surprise. Georgia threaded her way through the piles, attempting not to lose her footing.

A few yards beyond the book piles were a set of doors with push bars. The glass in the upper section of the doors had long been broken out and only wire remained in the frames. She threw her shoulder into the door on the right, expecting some resistance. There was none; it gave without any hesitation and she hurtled through the doorway, moving into the pool area with more momentum than she'd intended.

Slipping on the tile, she skidded to an eventual stop just shy of the edge of the pool and stood up. Surprisingly, there was still water in the pool. Georgia estimated there was only about a foot of it in there, but she imagined it was some form of insurance liability to have any in there at all. Glancing up, she saw the roof here was intact. The presence of the foul brown water was even more puzzling.

"Sarah? Valerie? Where are you guys?" she shouted, looking around.

She received no answer. The room was largely empty aside from the pool itself. There was more of the same style of graffiti on the walls of the room, similar to what had been in the common area. No furniture had been dumped in this room, at least around the perimeter. Anything junked in here had been thrown in the pool, she saw. The floats which had delineated the shallow and deep ends of the pool remained, still warning off less experienced swimmers from the more dangerous water.

Where else could they have gone? She turned and stared down the hallway which had led her here, which stood completely empty. There were no other rooms at the end of the hallway apart from the pool. She hadn't heard anything else as she had come through. They had to be in here. But she couldn't see anyone else in there. Frustrated, she took out the flashlight again.

Before she could switch it on, she heard a laugh behind her. It sounded smothered, as if the person had attempted to suppress it by putting a hand over their mouth. As she pivoted, she clicked the light on.

The beam erupted to life, illuminating the pool. Sitting in the center of the shallow end was an old, rusted wheelchair.

With a girl sitting in it.

A girl who was not Sarah, and was not Valerie.

CHAPTER TWENTY-ONE

It took several minutes to orient themselves on the second floor to find Room 244. The darkness made the search all the more difficult, never minding the fact that the majority of the numbers on the doors were no longer attached in many cases and, if they were, could not be accurately read. They had encountered one wing where all of the doors to the rooms had been removed.

Gregory's mood was peculiar. He was alternately furious at being obstructed in his search for the room and giddy to be looking for it. Jackson could see Sarah's frustration mounting as she attempted to keep up with the changes in his temperament.

Jackson was simply annoyed with him. While he had not been much of a fan to begin with, this behavior was too much. His insistence on locating his grandmother's cell was understandable to a degree, but getting angry about it wasn't helping anything. At this point, Jackson was out of patience and out of sorts. The more time he spent with Gregory, the less he understood Sarah's fondness for him. He came across as a supercilious and arrogant prick, his favorite pastime to make himself feel superior to everyone around him. Sarah, at least while they were dating, had never been that kind of person. Used to being one of the smartest people in a room, yes, but never to the point where she lorded her intelligence over anyone else. Unless she had begun becoming more like Gregory, he was unsure how long this relationship would last. It would have to get old after a while. Jackson was over it already and he wasn't even dating him.

As usual, Gregory led the way down the hall, flashlight pointed out in front of him like a weapon, forcing the inky blackness back. As in the other buildings, the dust and debris clouded the air as they moved, swirling about their feet as they stepped. Gregory's pace had slowed significantly as he was counting room numbers.

"240," he murmured, moving to the right to peer at a cell door. "We're almost there."

Jackson had been correct in his assessment of Sarah. Her patience was wearing thin. In the course of a day, she had seen a side of him which had been either hidden or nonexistent. His behavior since arriving at the hospital grounds had fluctuated almost constantly, from being condescending to officious to curious to angry.

One of the things which had originally attracted her to him had been his intelligence. He was easy on the eyes as well, that had been a positive too, but she had really taken to his mind first and foremost. They had met, of all places, in a bookstore.

She had been sitting in the café portion of the store, sipping idly and reading a book on philosophy a friend had recommended. The café had been packed, it being a Saturday afternoon, and all the other tables had been full. Gregory had approached her, coffee cup in one hand and a bag with a book purchase in the other, and had asked to take the open seat at her table. She'd eyed him skeptically at first but when she didn't sense a creepy vibe, had nodded and invited him to sit down. After a few moments of silence, he had struck up a conversation with her about her book, as he had read it a few months before. And that had been the start of it.

She had admired his brain and been puzzled by his relative lack of a sense of humor. He could not have been any less like Jackson if he had been purposely trying to.

And there were moments, not just a few of them, where she had wished Gregory possessed more of Jackson's sense of humor and personality.

Right now was one of them. Jackson was always even-keeled, never manic. He could always be counted on to have the cool head in any situation and had shown that again today. He was calm and pragmatic and Sarah missed that. She glanced at him as they paced one another down the dark hallway, trailing Gregory. He was as he always was – taking in his surroundings, calmly paying attention to everything and drinking it all in. His eyes weren't darting from place to place, his voice when speaking was unwavering.

When they got out of here, she and Gregory were going to have a long talk about his behavior. His tones were clipped and impatient. She was used to it on occasion with the rest of their friends because he believed he was smarter than they were. Maybe he was, but that didn't give him license to act like an asshole. He was generally an asshole when it came to Jackson, mainly due to jealousy and rivalry.

Part of Sarah liked that and took a bit of sick pleasure in it, especially since she and Jackson had remained friends. Not something to be proud of, she knew. It was shitty and petty, but perhaps now that she had acknowledged it, she wouldn't feel the need to do it any longer.

After seeing how today had gone, limiting Jackson and Gregory's interaction in the future would be in everyone's best interest. It had been unfair to both of them.

Jackson turned and looked back at Sarah, giving her a grim half-smile. The shadows cast strangely on his face, making him appear angry. She knew he wasn't and knew it was merely a trick of the light.

"So...come here often?" he asked jocularly, bumping his shoulder into hers and trying to ease the tension.

Sarah rolled her eyes. "Oh yes, all the time," she laughed. "I was thinking about moving in. It's almost like a resort, isn't it?"

"What are you two talking about?" Gregory asked from farther down the hall, carefully inspecting yet another doorway.

"Nothing," she answered sullenly. "Just making a joke. Never mind."

"Okay then," he dismissed. "I found her room." Now he was back to sounding excited all over again. He trailed his fingers delicately over the doorframe, swinging his body into the room. Jackson and Sarah looked at one another again briefly, and then moved forward in unison to the doorway.

There was nothing remarkable about it upon first glance. This cell was the carbon copy of all the others they had seen inside this building. Padded walls. Small window with the glass actually intact around the wire between the panes. There was no remaining furniture inside the room. The paint peeled from the ceiling, littering the floor. Whatever the walls had been made of looked dry and cracked and was devoid of graffiti. It was just...a room. It was merely an empty cell which had housed at least one murderer. Likely more than one, over the years.

The three of them stood in somber silence for a few minutes, none of them moving. Jackson shoved his hands into his pockets, unsure of what to do or say. He decided to stay in place until someone else spoke.

Sarah felt trapped in the same stasis, waiting to see what Gregory did next so she could merely react instead of initiate. As the seconds, and then minutes, ticked by, however, she grew less patient and finally could stay silent no longer.

"So...is it what you expected it would be?" she inquired, her tone light.

He grunted a laugh. "Well, I can't really say what I expected to find. I suppose part of me wanted her to have left some mark of herself in here, but that was extremely unlikely. I wish I had thought to bring my Ouija board with me."

She was surprised to hear that. "I didn't know you had one," she told him. "What on earth would you have done with it here?"

Gregory turned to look at her then, his face scornful. "Attempted to contact her, of course."

"But...why?"

"Why? That's a stupid question, Sarah. Can you imagine the things she would have been able to tell me?"

"Man, I don't think that's a good idea at all," Jackson stated.

"Why not?" Gregory asked haughtily.

"Well, for starters, that this place was full of crazy people. And you're assuming, of course, that ghosts and spirits are real. If they are, don't you think those spirits or whatever would be just as crazy in the afterlife as they were when they were here? And if the stories people tell about the living conditions in places like this are true, I'd bet those spirits would be pretty pissed off to be trapped here after they died."

"Regardless, thankfully you didn't bring one," Sarah sighed, grateful.

Gregory still looked unconvinced. "Well, I suppose I don't need one."

"That's what we were just saying," Jackson agreed, turning to step back out into the hallway.

"No, I mean I can make one."

That stopped him in his tracks. "What the hell are you talking about now?"

Gregory smiled, but it was all teeth and none of it kind. "I can make one. On the floor. I've heard of it being done before. I'd have to wing it with a planchette but I'm sure I could just use any old piece of paper to move around, and there's plenty of that here."

"But how would you make the board?" Sarah asked, aghast at the suggestion.

"Spray paint. On the floor. It's simple enough; I don't understand why the both of you keep asking questions. It's a simple yes, no, the alphabet, and a goodbye at the bottom. Easy enough."

"Where are you going to find spray paint?" Jackson felt like reality had taken a turn down a very bizarre street all of a sudden.

"I have a can in my bag."

"You have a can. Of spray paint. In your bag," Sarah stated slowly, enunciating each word.

"That's what I just said," he agreed.

"Why?"

"Why, what?" Irritation was increasing in his tone the more they spoke to him.

"Why do you have spray paint? Did you take up tagging as a hobby and didn't tell me or something?"

"No, of course not." He spit the words at her.

"Then why would you have brought it with you?"

Jackson watched this exchange, reluctant to add anything to the conversation. Sarah was fuming and he'd been on the receiving end of her temper more times than he could count. Gregory was on his own here.

"It seemed like a good idea. In case any of the buildings were difficult to navigate, we could put arrows on the walls for the direction we had come from or something."

"Uh huh." She still didn't seem convinced. "Well, that's fabulous. So if you're going to do some weirdo experiment with talking to your dead grandmother, I'm out. I've had enough, Gregory."

"Why?" It came out petulant, like a three-year-old who didn't get his way.

"Because we have been here all goddamn day. Our friends are in other buildings. One of them is injured and likely needs a doctor. I am tired. I am filthy. It's dark. I don't know how the fuck to get back to the car, and I have had enough. If you want to keep farting around in the dark and breathing in asbestos and potentially falling through a fucking floor while you talk to dead people, knock yourself out. But I'm leaving, Jackson is leaving, and we are going to find everyone else and go the fuck home."

Gregory's lips pursed in a moue of disappointment. "Do what you like. I'm staying for now. I want to check out a bit more of this building."

"So you're not going to make a Ouija board?" she asked.

"No. Mainly because I don't want to leave it for anyone else. I'll just have to come back another time and bring one with me instead." His face brightened. "Does that mean you'll stay and explore the rest of the building?"

Sarah was silent for a moment, pondering. "No." Jackson suppressed a sigh of relief. "We're still leaving. I just wanted to make sure you weren't going to go through with that terrible idea. I mean it – we're out of here. I'm going to call the others when we get out of the building. Are you sure you don't want to come too? It's really late. Louise is probably worried at this point."

"I'm sure. I want to see a bit more."

"All right then," Sarah said in defeat. She stepped over to him and kissed the corner of his mouth before turning around and walking out into the hallway. She stopped when she stepped over the threshold, turning her head toward the two men. "Coming, Jackson?"

Still unwilling to speak, he merely nodded and followed after her. He managed a small, halfhearted wave to Gregory as he stepped out of the room and into the hallway.

Gregory looked after them for a moment, hesitating. Part of him had had enough of the trip as well but the other part of him still wanted to see…more. There had to be more to this place than this dank, gray room. His grandmother had lived here, had spent uncounted hours within these four walls, full of madness and regret and mourning. Since he had first learned about her incarceration here for murdering her child, Gregory had been obsessed with learning more. He had researched all he could about her, about the hospital. He had peppered his family with questions about her, about the murder, about what her life in the hospital might have been like. This was his opportunity to try to find out more and he was reluctant to give up on that because his girlfriend and her friends were tired and bored.

"Fuck that," he said, and turned back toward the room, staring out the window at the rear wall.

CHAPTER TWENTY-TWO

Jay turned from the row of cabinets he had been inspecting, frowning as he did so. He had gone through every cabinet and every drawer he could find in the room and had not found much. He supposed this was due to their being Johnny-Come-Lately's to the site. Everything had either been moved offsite or had been picked over by others looking to take home a souvenir. There was not an instrument or bunch of papers to be found in this room. He had searched several others and had been equally disappointed. Moving toward the door, he wondered if Val had had any luck.

Stepping into the hallway, he called for her. Hearing no answer, he began to shine his light into the oncoming doorways. After having no luck in three rooms farther down the hallway, he paused for a moment. He didn't recall seeing or hearing her pass by and remembered having turned a corner to come to this section of the building. He turned and headed in the direction from where they had originally come. She must have gotten caught up in another room. He called to her again, hoping for an answer.

Yet again, he received no response. He called louder but heard only the echo of his own voice, which sounded frightened. His flashlight did little to illuminate the surrounding darkness and he found himself wishing he had brought more than one with him, or perhaps one to have worn on his head. Hindsight was pointless – as his mother liked to say, you could shit in one hand and wish in the other and see which one filled up first. No amount of wishing would provide him with any additional lights and it was extraordinarily unlikely that any previous explorers had left any in the building. He had what he had and that would have to do.

"Val?" he called again into the echoing dark. "You up here?" Maybe she was annoyed that he was taking so long and had gone back outside to wait. Jay realized he had reached the staircase where he had come up with no sign of her anywhere. She had to have left the building entirely or maybe back into the rooms on the first floor, though that seemed unlikely. Or maybe she *had* passed him in the hallway and he had been too engrossed or looking in the wrong direction when she had gone by.

Jay could feel anxiety rising within him and he stopped at the stairwell to take stock and make a plan. Valerie could be downstairs or outside, but she could also be in the rooms beyond where he had searched. If she had passed him, she had done so without looking for him first or calling out to him. The same if she had decided to leave the building and head outside. Even if she had been pissed at him for taking too long, it was unlikely she would have just up and left. Val was not the kind of girl who kept her anger locked up. If she had been angry, Jay would have known about it. Loudly.

Inhaling deep, he blew the breath out noisily, and began walking back down the hallway again.

Counting doors was pointless, he realized. In heading first in one direction and then doubling back, he had lost track of exactly which one he had been in originally or where he had stopped searching. Frustrated, he began shining his light into all of them and repeatedly shouting Val's name as he moved.

This was ridiculous. It wasn't as if this was one of the larger buildings, it was actually comparatively small. This should have been the one place they explored which would have been the least likely to lose track of anyone. And yet, here he was, yelling like a jackass as panic bubbled in his stomach as each room turned up empty.

Coming to the last room, which looked vaguely familiar, he noted there were only two more doors remaining before the hallway dead ended, a large window with the glass broken out showing the end of the road. Either she was in one of these rooms or she had, in fact, gone out and not told him. He shined the flashlight into the room ahead of him, passing it from one side to the next. Just another empty laboratory, identical cabinets along one side and no other furniture inside. One down, one to go, he told himself, moving forward in the hallway to the last door.

Light licked over debris on the floor, fallen paint chips and plaster, much like every other location Jay had seen since they arrived. His boots crunched as he took another step into the last room. The center of the room held an overturned gurney. He saw a filing cabinet in one corner, its drawers partially open. Nothing remarkable thus far.

Swinging the light to the left corner, an examination table came into view. An examination table that was not empty. There was a figure atop the table. Jay's heart quickened in his chest.

"Val?" he questioned. "What, did you decide to take a nap or something?" If she had, this certainly should have woken her up. She hadn't even stirred. "Val?" he called again, sprinting into the room and to the table.

He held his light aloft to get a better view. She wasn't napping.

Jay moved the light from her legs up to her torso. She wasn't just lying on the exam table; she was bound to it with canvas restraints. Bound. Her legs *and* her arms. Something she would not have been able to do on her own.

Continuing to move the light, it finally rested on her face, which was frozen in a silent scream, her eyes wide and unseeing.

"Valerie!" he screamed, almost dropping the flashlight to the floor. Fumbling, he placed it in the crook of his armpit so he could work on the restraints. He was still screaming, yelling into her face, trying to get some response out of her.

His fingers worked furiously at the buckles on the restraints on her arms. When he finally worked them both free, he grabbed her shoulders, shaking her. Still her mouth remained in the shape of an O; her eyes were unblinking and bloodshot. He placed a hand to her face against her cheek. Her skin was smooth and cool to the touch. No heat, no warmth, no life. With a hitching sob, he brought the light up and shined it directly onto her face.

Her pupils did not retract, they were fixed and dilated. She had what looked like a burn at her temple. Jay turned her head toward him, seeing an identical mark on the opposite. His knees buckled and he slumped, the upper half of his body crumpling atop hers, his cries muffled by the bunching of her shirt at her waist.

How? How had this happened to her? He hugged her tight to him, unwilling to believe she was gone. Who had done this? She could not have restrained herself onto the table and she sure as hell hadn't been able to give herself those marks on her head. Someone else was in this building with them. But who? And why would they have hurt his Valerie? She didn't have a mean bone in her body. She wept every time one of those animal cruelty commercials with the sad music came on the television. How could she be dead? How could someone have killed her?

A sound behind him. Footsteps coming down the hallway. He could hear the crunch of the dirt and broken glass as they moved closer. Relief flooded through him. Perhaps someone else could help her. At the very least, they would be able to get out of here and find help. Jay rose to his feet. "Oh, thank god," he wailed, turning toward the doorway, expecting to see Jackson or Sarah or Adam.

"I don't think you should be thanking him just yet," rasped a voice in response.

CHAPTER TWENTY-THREE

Massive glass fixtures in the roof let in moonlight, which reflected off the brackish water in the pool. The room was still, the water smooth as glass. Georgia had retreated against the rear wall; her eyes open wide in disbelief. Her arms were spread apart, palms flat against the cool tiled wall as she stared. And stared. She was afraid to move, afraid to speak a word.

She did not recognize the girl who was seated, unmoving, in the wheelchair. The girl was frail, emaciated arms pulled up toward her chest. Her legs were equally thin, accentuating each bone's outline with the lack of fat or muscle. Stringy brown hair hid the majority of her facial features from Georgia, but she was able to discern wide, brown eyes behind the locks. Was this some kind of joke? Had this girl come in here for the same purpose as Georgia and her friends - to explore? Perhaps she had heard the rest of them moving around the buildings throughout the afternoon and, with a sick sense of humor, had planted herself here to scare them? The other alternative which crossed Georgia's mind was that maybe the girl was a squatter, camping out here to hide from the rest of the world, where there were no bills to pay or landlords to hide from.

Georgia noticed the girl's attire – definitely not street clothes. They resembled something closer to a hospital gown, exposing her legs but covering her torso. The fabric had been light in color originally but now was covered in an assortment of stains. Her feet were bare, causing Georgia to lean more toward the squatter theory.

"Hello?" she said, feeling ridiculous but obviously needing to say *something* to the girl. They had spotted one another and Georgia couldn't bring herself to just stand there in silence, waiting one another out to see who would speak first.

The other girl did not answer. She merely continued to sit unnervingly still, peering out at Georgia through the veil of hair. Georgia felt at a loss. What the hell did she do next? She remembered Adam, poor Adam, in Building 51, all alone. She had gone in search of help. Maybe this girl could provide it, doubtful as it seemed.

"I need your help," she pleaded, though did not move from her position against the wall. "My friends are somewhere in one of the other buildings and I can't find them and my cell phone won't work. My boyfriend is…hurt, he got hurt in one of the buildings and oh, god, I need to get him some help. Do you have a cell phone that works? I can't get a signal on mine. Have you seen anyone else come through this building tonight? I thought I heard my friends in here but now I can't find them. Can you help me?" The words all spilled out in a rush, a torrent of anxiety and worry she had been holding inside while she had been searching for the others. Her eyes welled with tears, hoping she would be able to find everyone else and get back to Adam.

The girl in the wheelchair did not respond to her entreaty for assistance, she did not speak a word. She raised one of her hands to her face and with a spidery white finger, pushed a lock of her hair back behind her ear. More of her features were revealed to Georgia, and the sight was unsettling. Her skin was alabaster, and not in a complimentary model fashion. It was white in the way that weathered bone was white, or someone who had been locked away to never see the sun was white. She possessed sunken cheeks and pale, bloodless lips on an emotionless face with dark circles under her eyes. Georgia was unable to determine her age; she could have been anywhere between fifteen and thirty.

She tried again. "Can you please help me?" Georgia cried. "I need to get help for my boyfriend. Please?"

No reply. The thin arm raised again to the face, spidery finger this time moving in front of the thin mouth in a "shh" gesture. Georgia could see what appeared to be a thin, plastic bracelet around her small wrist. The kind she had worn when she'd had her appendix removed. The kind hospitals put on patients. Her heart raced, blood flowing cold in her veins.

The girl shifted in her seat slightly, making the brown water surrounding her ripple out to the edges of the pool. Her lips began to move, her voice barely above a whisper. "Help. You need help." A slight nodding of the head in understanding. "I need help. I have been waiting for help."

Georgia's eyes squinted as she strained to listen and comprehend what she was saying. "You need help? What happened to you?" She took a few inquisitive steps away from the wall, closer to the edge of the pool so she could hear the girl better.

The girl in the wheelchair nodded. "Yes, I need help. I don't swim very well. I needed help in the pool." She glanced down, breaking eye contact.

"But if you don't swim well, why are you in the water? I mean, there can't be much in there, but why would you want to be in the water? It looks filthy. Come out of there and we'll get help together," Georgia encouraged, gesturing for the girl to come to her.

"I wanted to learn to swim, I really did," the girl continued, her voice mournful. "I wanted to do the backstroke. The backstroke always looked so calm. And in here, you could look out the ceiling and see the sky. You could swim under all the clouds. It was like being outside. But I needed extra help because I was afraid of the water." She shifted again in the wheelchair, drawing her knees up closer to her chest, drawing her body into a protective ball. Her hair loosed itself from being tucked behind her ear and fell forward, obscuring her face once again.

Georgia did not know at all what to make of this conversation. Obviously there was something wrong with her, but this was the first person she had been able to find in this place in what felt like hours. She couldn't just walk away from her now. Granted, she was growing impatient at the time they were wasting but she felt as though she didn't have another choice but to listen.

"Why were you afraid of the water?" she asked, hoping if she kept her talking and got this story out they could move on and find her friends.

"Daddy gave me a bath once," the girl in the wheelchair replied. "He put me in the bathtub and told me to get all clean and then he would put me to bed. So I did what Daddy told me to, I always did what Daddy told me to. I was a good girl. But I made a mistake and I dropped the shampoo into the water and it spilled and broke. There was soap all over and I made a mess. Daddy was mad. He got all shouty and his face was all red. He said I was a bad girl, a no good girl, a stupid girl who would never do anything right. He got all red like a tomato from all the yelling and he hit me. Good girls don't break things. I was a good girl but not that night, no. That night I was a bad and stupid girl, and Daddy punished me."

Georgia once again found herself stepping closer to the pool again to hear her. The hair on her arms stood at attention, transfixed by the story. The toes of her boots were inches shy of the edge. The girl began to speak again in the same dry, whispering tone.

"Daddy pushed my face right down in that water. I couldn't breathe; I couldn't get my head out. I tried to lift my head to get a breath but all I got was water. I choked and spit but all I could breathe was the water. I don't remember much after that, it all went dark and quiet. And then I woke up in the hospital. Everything there was white and it smelled funny, like chemicals. The brightness made my eyes hurt and I just cried and cried. I wanted to tell Daddy that I was sorry. Except Daddy wasn't there. It was just my mommy and she said I would never see Daddy again because he had hurt me real bad and I would never be better and Daddy had to go away where they put bad people."

Jesus Christ, Georgia thought to herself. "I'm so sorry. What happened then?" she asked, trying to move her along, hating herself for doing so.

The girl in the wheelchair raised her head, looking directly at Georgia. Her hair fell back, exposing her face fully for the first time. Now that she was standing closer to the edge of the pool, Georgia could see the anger blaze in her eyes.

"I came here. This was a bad place. A bad place with bad doctors and bad people. Lots of shots. Lots of pills. Lots of people to poke you. Lots of people to do bad things to you. But sometimes we did okay things. Like movies, sometimes. Or like this pool. I wanted to learn to swim," she repeated, looking down to the water forlornly. "Mostly, I would come here and sit in a chair on the side and watch everyone else swim. It looked like so much fun. I wanted to do it, too. I wanted to have fun. After a while, I thought maybe I would try. I would stand in the water where it didn't go too high on my legs, where my face wasn't near the water. And everyone else could do their swimming but I would just stand in the water."

With a speed Georgia would not have thought possible, the girl in the wheelchair sprang forth, seeming to glide across the shallow water instead of moving through it. She reached out, grasping Georgia's arm and pulled her off balance. Georgia fell forward, into the pool.

The water was shallow, only a bit over two feet deep where she fell. The girl from the wheelchair's hold was vise-like, and she twisted Georgia's arm behind her back. Georgia crouched, her arm screaming in protest. It took her a moment to recover from her surprise before she began to struggle. While she tried to wriggle free, the girl began to speak again.

"Oh, I stood in the water while the other people swam," she hissed through gritted teeth. "Until they started to laugh at me that I was afraid. They called me a scaredy cat, even the lifeguard people. Scaredy cat, that's what I was. And the other people thought it would be funny to splash me. And they splashed and splashed and my hair got wet and I started to cry. And the more I cried, the more they laughed at me. It's not nice to laugh at people," she lectured Georgia as she changed her stance for better leverage. "You shouldn't do that. It's mean. But they kept laughing. And they splashed me more. And then they did the meanest thing, they did like my daddy. They pushed me under water. Just. Like. This."

Georgia sputtered as the cold, brackish water hit her face, closing over her eyes, her nose, and her mouth. She struggled harder against the girl, who stood behind her, pushing her head down with one hand as the other held fast to her arm. She tried to kick out the girl's legs but was unable to connect with either of them. She held her breath, her chest burning. The disturbance in the water had kicked up debris which had settled to the bottom. She could feel dead leaves caressing her face as they floated by.

She opened her eyes, expecting not to be able to see anything in the dark water. Surprisingly, the water was clear as day. The bottom was easily visible, the pebbled concrete clean. The water stung her eyes, the same sensation as being in her parents' swimming pool as a child, searching the bottom for a sunken toy. Georgia could hear other sounds around her, muffled through the water. It wasn't the girl speaking above her, this was different. It was multiple voices, not a solitary one. It sounded like laughter.

Jennifer L. Place 112

"No one helped me," the girl went on to say, undaunted by Georgia's thrashing. "I screamed for help and no one helped me. So I'm not going to help you." With a rush of force, she pushed Georgia's head farther under the water, until Georgia's cheek met the bottom of the pool with a rough scrape.

Georgia screamed then, both from the pain of the scrape and the fright of being farther under water. The scream was soundless above water. The only evidence was a flotilla of bubbles as she released air from her lungs into the water. Her lungs were on fire, her muscles burned from the effort of struggling. She was unable to break the hold on her arm, unable to move from the hand holding her under. Her eyes opened, bulging from lack of oxygen. The water was so murky; she was unable to see anything but blackness.

The blackness was unchanged when her lungs, unable to refrain any longer, breathed in the water from the pool.

When the struggles ceased, the girl released her hold on Georgia and glided back to her wheelchair, where she took up the same position Georgia had found her in when she had entered the pool. After a moment, her body shimmered, then became transparent, then disappeared altogether.

All that remained in the room was the rusty wheelchair and Georgia's body, floating in the shallow end of the murky pool.

CHAPTER TWENTY-FOUR

Sarah and Jackson made their way down the stairs from the second floor of Ryon Hall. Neither of them said much, their only interest in getting out of the building. Sarah was perplexed by Gregory's behavior and Jackson wasn't sure what to say about it. He was in the unenviable position of having an opinion on how Gregory had treated her. Being her ex-boyfriend as well as her friend, he had to walk a fine line in how much truth he actually spoke aloud. A conversation was coming, and he was thankful to have the walk out of the building to consider his words before it happened.

They wound their way through the hallways to get back to the entrance to the basement. Jackson had considered trying one of the actual doors to see if they could exit that way instead of going back through the basement but thought better of it. The main door had been securely blocked and he had the suspicion that the others would have been as well. Instead, they trudged back down into the bowels of the building. Sarah kept pace behind him as he had insisted upon going first. Chivalry might be ailing but it certainly wasn't dead yet.

The halls were silent but for their footsteps as they passed through the final hallway to the basement door. They were both on edge despite the stillness and were eager to be outside in the fresh air. Jackson preceded her down the stairs, his flashlight finding the broken window they had entered through previously. They both stopped just shy of the window, realizing it would be more difficult to get out than it had to get in. While the height to the window wasn't terribly far, it was high enough to be prohibitive. Neither was confident in their upper body strength to get them back out without issue. Jackson shone his light around the room, looking for something suitable to get a leg up for the exit.

His light came to rest on an old wheelchair parked beside a filing cabinet. "What do you think?" he asked Sarah, leaving the light on the chair so she could see it.

She shrugged, and then realized he would be unable to see the shrug in the darkness. "I guess that should be fine," she agreed half-heartedly. "I doubt there's a stepladder anywhere around here that we're going to find. Just remember to turn the brakes on. I don't feel like flying across the room in a runaway chair."

Jackson barked out a short laugh, a staccato burst in the still air. "Of course. I'll remember to turn the brake on for you. I'll even be a gentleman and let you go first."

"That's big of you," she replied. "I appreciate the gesture. You're too kind."

Jackson stepped over to where the wheelchair stood, pushing it by the handles toward the window. As instructed, he stepped on the brakes on the wheels to prevent it from sliding out from under their weight. He stepped back, flashlight tucked into his armpit, and bowed toward Sarah, inviting her to climb up and then out.

She curtsied, and indicated for him to hold the chair steady while she climbed aboard. She tested the strength of the leather seat with one foot before daring to put all of her weight on the chair. She didn't want to have the material give and end up breaking an ankle if her foot was to go straight through it. It appeared sound and she stepped onto the seat with both of her feet, clinging to the bottom of the window with her hands.

The concrete was cold and unyielding under her palms, the grit digging into the soft skin. She took a deep breath before heaving herself upward. She hoisted her head and shoulders up into the open window, bracing her arms against the sides, and shimmied the rest of her body up and out. It was as dark outside on the grounds as it had been inside the basement. Sarah scooted backward and kneeled in front of the open window. "Come on out," she commanded Jackson, just shy of a whisper.

A few seconds later, his arms and head emerged from the window, appearing in the soft moonlight as if the building was giving birth to him. His shoulders followed and he slithered out of the window just as she had. They both stood after a moment, brushing dirt from their clothes. They looked around, taking stock of what they were able to see in the dark.

Nothing moved. All was quiet. Neither had ever been in a situation quite like this before; the sight of what amounted to its own small village left to rot with no electricity was an experience which neither could accurately articulate. What Sarah found to be most disturbing, odd as it would have seemed to try to explain to Jackson, were the streetlights. Regular, old streetlights which could be found along any road in any town. There were many of them strewn about where the old roads had been. They all stood as dark sentries, many with vines clinging from top to bottom. She couldn't say how long it had been since they had the ability to perform their intended function. It was sad and creepy at the same time. They were surrounded by massive buildings with no light coming from any windows. The only light came from the moon itself, which hung heavy in the sky above. Occasionally, it shone through broken windows of surrounding edifices, outlining strange shapes in those buildings which had trees growing within them where the roofs had fallen in.

Sarah rubbed her upper arms with her hands, trying to stifle the shudder the place was giving her. "What should we do?" she asked, looking at Jackson anxiously.

He thought a moment before answering. "Well, I guess we have two real choices. We can go back to the buildings we were in before and round up the others where we left them, or we can try to find the power plant again on our own and then go back to Louise's. I can't think of any other options, really. Who knows how long Gregory will be in that building contemplating Ouija boards and talking to the spirits."

Sarah frowned but Jackson was unsure whether it was from their dismal options of what to do or in response to his remark about Gregory. He supposed it could be both.

"We'd be pretty shitty friends if we just took off without them," she stated, speaking slowly.

He knew what she really wanted to do was get the hell out of there as quickly as their feet could carry them, but guilt would make them both go back to where they had left their friends. "I suppose we would be," he concurred, nodding slowly. "So I guess we go find Jay and Val first then, since we left their building last. Then we'll go back to Building 51 and get Georgia and Adam."

She sighed heavily. Jackson heard the zipper of her bag open as she took out a bottle of water and took a drink. He heard the zipper again as she closed the bag back up. "I guess we'd better get moving.

The sun will be coming back up by the time we find them and then get the hell out of here. It feels like we've been in here for days."

Jackson nodded his agreement. He took in their surroundings, getting his bearings. "The morgue is over that way," he told her, gesturing toward his right. "Let's go get Valerie and Jay." He started off in the direction he had indicated and Sarah followed obediently behind him.

They walked in silence for a minute or two before Jackson felt as though he needed to say something. "Sarah," he began, speaking slowly as his brain still considered how to put his words together properly.

"Don't," she interrupted him, not turning to look at him. She continued walking along, chin up but fixed straight ahead. "I know what you're going to say and it's not worth having the conversation."

"Oh, you know what I'm going to say? When did you notice the psychic behavior? Was it always there or did you recently develop it?" he answered, unable to keep the edge of sarcasm out of his voice.

She sighed. "Yes, I know what you're going to say and no, I'm not psychic. You're just predictable. You're going to tell me that Gregory is an asshole."

"Well, I'd like to think I would have put it a bit more elegantly than that," Jackson retorted, mildly offended.

"Oh, I'm sure you would have said it delicately, but the subtext would have been there. That he's an asshole. That he shouldn't have spoken the way he did, that he appears to be a little too focused on this place."

"Well, I suppose that's not entirely inaccurate, but…"

"And you're right."

"Wait, what?"

She laughed lightly and finally turned to meet his gaze. Despite the darkness, Jackson could see the shimmer of tears in her eyes. "You're right," she repeated, shrugging her shoulders. "I care about Gregory but when you get right down to it, he's kind of a dick. That's not shocking news to me, he's been condescending since I met him. It was almost endearing. But seeing him today and his...I don't know, *need* to be here and explore this place and try to communicate with his crazy dead grandmother, well, it's a side of him I hadn't seen before and I can't say I really like. He's been a dick all day and the whole Ouija board thing...I don't even know what to say."

Jackson was taken aback by her forthrightness. He had expected anger, a bit of swearing, and lots of insults hurled at him about what an asshole he had been when they had dated and then broken up. This was not the answer he had anticipated and now was almost speechless in its wake. He realized they had stopped walking. "There's probably not much else *to* say, I suppose," he stated, mulling over her words. "You basically said it all right there. The only other thing I can think to ask is – what are you going to do about it?"

Sarah pondered the question before answering. "I honestly don't know," she replied. "I care about him, sure, but if this is the real him, the real Gregory, the one who's going to be a dick to me, talk to my friends as if they're morons, and be convinced he can spray-paint words onto a floor to talk to dead mental patients...well, that sounds like I don't really have many options."

"I'd have to agree with you there," Jackson acquiesced, happy to hear her ability to see the situation rationally.

"This, of course, does not mean you and I are getting back together," she cautioned him, turning to give him a sidelong grin.

"The thought never crossed my mind," he stated, though of course it *had* crossed his mind. Now certainly was not the time for them to discuss the possibility, however slight. When they had worked, they had worked really well. When they hadn't worked, they'd had fights of epic proportions, though that had made things all the more exciting. Neither of them did anything halfway. He'd table the subject for now. And perhaps they were better off as friends. He was becoming accustomed to being a bachelor and Sarah would, of course, want to be alone for a bit. But this was a good situation for her.

Jackson had made the effort to be civil to Gregory and he had kept his word. In the end, Gregory had shot himself in the foot just by his very nature of needing to be the smartest in the room. That trait got old after a while, no matter the company.

They continued their trek back to the morgue, gravel and dead sticks crackling under their feet. The night was close around them, the moonlight affording little more than the outlines of objects surrounding them. The thrill of fear every time there was a sound nearby had waned; Jackson had rationalized it to the fact that nighttime creatures were unlikely to curtail their activities simply because the two of them were trespassing on their territory. He imagined there was a lively population of deer, raccoons and opossums on the grounds and in the woods which encircled the property. The occasional owl hooted from the tree line and bats swirled in the sky above them.

Arriving at the morgue, Jackson paused before the structure, hesitating. The way in was at the rear of the building, where they had gained entrance previously, but he had stopped walking at the front. His eyes scanned the windows of the different floors, straining to see any indication of moving flashlight beams and trying to hear any sounds of human occupation.

Sarah looked at him quizzically. "What are you doing?" she asked, eyes narrowed in confusion.

"Trying to see if I can spot them in there."

"Do you have x ray vision now or something?"

"No, but since there's no electricity in there, I thought maybe I'd be able to see flashlight beams if they were moving around inside."

"Well, that's all well and good so long as they're close to this side of the building," she countered. "Not so much if they're in the back."

"Touché," Jackson agreed. "So then, let's go in." He stepped off toward the rear entrance, Sarah following.

The door was still ajar from when they had left Jay and Valerie. He stopped again to look at the windows at the rear as he had done at the front of the building. Sounds were coming from above, scuffling sounds and muffled howls. Jackson and Sarah both turned their heads in that direction, still not seeing any lights. "What the fuck?" he asked wonderingly, unable to look away.

CHAPTER TWENTY-FIVE

Jay spun around to find the source of the voice. Standing a few paces away, blocking his exit from the room, was a hunched, filthy man. His clothes might have been white originally, but Jay thought that time had long since passed. Arms that seemed too long for the frame extended out from the short shirtsleeves, tapered fingers at the end of overly large hands. Had the man been standing erect, he would have likely exceeded six and a half feet. His build was slight, his stooped stature appearing as if his head was too heavy for him to stand upright.

"Who the hell are you?" Jay exclaimed, more out of surprise than fear.

The question seemed to give the man pause, as if he had to consider the answer before speaking. His face was hidden from Jay's prying eyes as the man stared at the floor, not looking directly at Jay.

"Kevin. I'm Kevin," the dirty man announced, his voice wavering slightly with uncertainty.

"Did you do this to her?" Jay asked, snapping out of his surprise and pointing down at Valerie's prone form. "Did you kill her?"

Still looking at the floor, the man shook his head. "No. No, no, no, no."

"Then who did? Who the fuck else is here?" It took every bit of restraint for Jay not to scream. He wanted to take him by the shoulders and shake until answers fell out of him.

The man laughed, a sound unnervingly similar to a door being opened on rusty hinges. It sounded out of practice and simply wrong. "That is an excellent question," the dirty man praised him. "Who is here? Am I here? Are you here?"

"What are you talking about? Who else is on these grounds? Who killed my girlfriend?"

The man shuffled a few steps closer to Jay and to the table upon which Valerie lay. His head moved in a rapid jerking motion, giving the table a glance before turning back again to the floor. "That would be the work of the good doctor," he informed Jay, his body quaking slightly at the mention.

"Who the hell is that?" Jay countered. Was this man some leftover patient who had nowhere to go and squatted here on the grounds? This wasn't going anywhere. It was too late for Valerie and he knew it. But somehow he needed to get out and get help. They all needed to get out of here, the sooner the better.

"The doctor. It was the doctor. The doctor," Kevin kept repeating, over and over, each recitation seeming to pain him, so much so that he brought his huge hands up to the sides of his head, clutching at it as though it might burst apart if he didn't hold it together. "The doctor, the doctor," he continued to intone, almost moaning it now.

Jay was unsure how to either engage this man in intelligible conversation or how to escape him. He was trapped here, with the other man standing in the doorway. He needed out, he thought again, they all did. But it seemed as though he would not be going anywhere anytime soon. Trying again to extract information, he struggled to find a calmer tone. "Who is the doctor? What did he do to Valerie? Did he do something to you?"

This only seemed to upset Kevin further and he began to shake his head from side to side, stringy hair swaying to and fro with the motion. "Supposed to help me," he grunted, eyes shut tight, hands still gripping the sides of his head.

"And he didn't help you?" Jay employed the same soothing voice, hoping this was leading somewhere productive but not holding out too much hope.

"No," the word came out as a sob, the narrow chest hitching with each breath. The man's tall frame leaned heavily against the doorway, his eyes hidden behind a lanky arm as he continued to cry.

Jay took a tentative step toward him, arms out before him in a gesture of peace. "It's all right," he whispered, moving forward another step. "Is the doctor still here now?"

Jennifer L. Place   122

Kevin shook his head again, only identifiable by the movement of his hair. He continued to weep against the doorframe, his face still concealed by his folded arms.

"All right," Jay said, straightening up and exhaling. "Then you and I will get out of here and we'll find some help. Do you want to come with me, Kevin? Can you help me find my way out of here?"

The man only sobbed louder, sounding more pathetic to Jay than a child who dropped its ice cream cone on the sidewalk. He was filled with pity for this ungainly and obviously disturbed man, who clearly had little idea where he was or what to do with himself. Jay knew enough about the closure of mental hospitals around the country years ago, their funding slashed and many of them, like this one, being forced to close their doors. This meant unleashing their patients upon the world, a world that did not accept them and which had no patience or understanding for their specific needs. They were bogeymen to most people, the type of people you barred your doors against. The kind they made movies about, who his around every corner, machete in hand, to murder horny teenagers

In truth, many were quite docile but the structure and routine of the hospitals were all they knew. When that familiarity was gone, many tried to come back and live in the abandoned buildings.

Despite his fear and his heartbreak over Valerie, if he could help and get Kevin out of here at the same time, he would do so. He didn't want to leave the distraught man here on his own.

Jay took another tentative step toward him, reaching out one hand to touch the other man's arm. Kevin jerked back as if he'd been burned, stepping back into the hallway. His head came up, eyes blazing with rage.

"No!" he repeated, though this time it was a roar instead of a sob. The sadness was gone, replaced now by fury. Jay was unsure what had brought on the swift change in demeanor, but he stumbled in his surprise, his body tilting forward toward Kevin He reached out with his arms in an effort to steady himself, again catching onto the other man.

This only enraged the man further. His eyes were wild and he continued to shout, "No!" over and over again, as he had before. He swung his arms back and forth, as if he was pumping them while sprinting. He struck Jay with one of them, knocking him to the floor of the hallway. Jay landed in a pile of dust, garbage and paint chips, sprawling out before Kevin's large feet, clad in tattered slip-on shoes. He attempted to get to his feet but now Kevin was in a sheer panic and kicked out, hitting Jay squarely in the collarbone.

Jay felt a flash of pain and cried out. All other instincts fled and now escape was his only motivation. Kevin continued to flail about, screaming unintelligibly. Jay was able to scoot himself backward far enough to be out of reach of his kicking legs. His right arm was useless, his collarbone surely broken. He drew his legs up so he was kneeling on the floor, the bulk of his weight on his left arm. Keeping his eyes on Kevin, he managed to pull himself up to a standing position, bracing himself against the wall, paint peeling beneath his fingers as they searched for purchase.

He was breathing heavily, pain hot and quick as it surged through his shoulder and arm. Where to go? Once he was able to take stock of his current position, he noticed that he was trapped. Kevin again stood between him and exiting the building. Instead of being trapped inside the room where Valerie had been murdered, now he was trapped at the end of a hallway. Kevin stood in the center of the hallway toward the stairs where Jay had gained access to this floor. The only thing behind Jay now was a window, nothing else. No more rooms to hide in, no other staircase leading back down to the first floor. This was it. End of the line. He was unsure if he could calm Kevin back down again to be able to go down the hallway. Never in his life had he seen a man behave like a whirling dervish.

Kevin was clawing at his head again, fingers biting deep into the flesh of his temples, under his eyes. He moaned and cried, still not saying any actual words Jay could understand. His legs periodically kicked out at nothing at all, in a constant state of movement.

Desperate and out of options, he began to move toward Kevin, toward the end of the hallway which held the promise of escape. If he could slip past the other man while he was engrossed in his fit or spasm or whatever this was, he could make a break for the stairs and freedom.

Jay backed up against the wall, sliding along its length and sloughing off paint as he went. He tried to make his movements as soundless as possible so as not to draw any attention. He marveled at Kevin's state as the man continued to jerk his legs and claw at his face. He was doing real damage now. Jay could see rivulets of blood sluicing down the man's sallow cheeks and streaming down the tops of his hands through his fingers. His cries fluctuated between shrieks and groans but all had ceased to be actual words, they were merely guttural and unintelligible.

Keeping his eyes pinned to Kevin's movements, Jay slunk along the wall toward the stairs. Focused solely on the other man, he kicked an empty, long forgotten beer bottle with his left foot, sending it skittering down the hallway. The clanging sound brought Kevin's immediate attention.

The man stood stock still, fixing his gaze upon Jay, who stopped moving immediately, frightened as a rabbit spotted by a fox. There were bloody half moons in the meat below Kevin's eyes, angry wounds still weeping blood down his face. Tendrils of greasy hair adhered to his cheeks, furthering his menacing visage. His chest rose and fell rapidly with each breath. His hands rose, arm bent at the elbow, his fingers clenched like bloody claws. He began to pivot in Jay's direction, cutting him off from the stairway.

Jay put out his good hand in a warding off gesture. "Kevin, just calm down," he began to say, attempting to keep the panic from his voice and knowing the effort failed as he heard the waver in his words. "The doctor isn't here anymore. Let's go downstairs and get some help, okay? You've hurt yourself and we should get that taken care of."

"I didn't hurt myself!" Kevin wailed, throwing his head back. "The doctor hurt me!" He snapped his head back, eyes rolling in their sockets as they focused back on Jay, a terrible gleam in them now. Through gritted, rotting teeth he spoke again. "And you...you're probably helping him. How many people have *you* hurt? How many?"

Terrified now, Jay began to move backward, trying to put more distance between himself and the disturbed man. "I don't know the doctor, Kevin. I haven't hurt anyone. The doctor hurt my girlfriend, Kevin, remember? She was lying on that table back there. He didn't just hurt her, he killed her. Why don't we both go out together and we'll get help. We'll find someone to help us and make sure the doctor doesn't hurt anyone else, okay?" His hip bumped into something unforgiving and his movement was halted. Jay spared a moment's glance to see that, while he had managed to put distance between himself and the other man, he had run out of room. He was now backed against the far wall. During his speech, he had made it to the window. He was out of hallway, out of choices. Looking quickly at the window, he saw this one no longer had the casement of a screen or bars on the outside, the metal having long ago rusted and fallen away. Could he make the jump down to the ground? What floor was he even on, the third? There was nothing down there to break his fall; there was no fire escape out of this window. He'd probably break a leg, if not both of them.

What other choice did he have? He had to act, and he had to do it now. Taking advantage of Kevin's inaction, Jay turned and smashed his left fist into the glass of the window. It shuddered in its frame but did not break. He sobbed in frustration and drew back his arm to strike again, sweat beading his brow in his fear.

Before his fist made its second impact, Jay felt a hand close on the collar of his shirt, drawing him backward. With a roar, Kevin hauled Jay toward him, shouting at him, spittle spraying into his face. "I knew it! I knew you were bad, too! I won't let you hurt me, too!" Kevin grabbed a handful of the waist of Jay's jeans with his free hand, and dragged him back to the window. "You're not gonna hurt me any…more!"

As if he was brandishing a battering ram, Kevin pulled his arms back, alarmingly strong for a man who appeared so frail, and thrust Jay's body forward, head first, into the window. The glass shattered this time, shards lacerating Jay's forehead and scalp. "I don't know the doctor!" Jay screamed at him, blood pouring into his eyes, obscuring his vision. Everything was merely a red haze. His eyes were full of blood and his mouth was full of terror and vomit.

Kevin drew him back again for another blow. This time, he moved his body slightly toward the right, toward the side of the window frame where jagged shards of glass remained in the frame.

It was for the best that Jay did not see it coming.

The glass flayed his cheek from eyes to chin and gouged his neck heavily, slicing through the flesh cleanly, quickly.

Then he was airborne, finally free of the hallway, of the disturbed, ruined man who had pegged him for an accomplice of the doctor who had murdered Valerie. His body hit the ground with an empty, unremarkable thud. He had been right; he had broken a leg on the way down. The leg was the least of his worries, though he barely felt it.

The worries were all fleeting, as it only took a few short minutes for him to die. His life drained away, pooling onto the dirty ground. His eyes, unseeing, were fixed upon the window above.

CHAPTER TWENTY-SIX

There was a moment of still silence, of paralysis, before Jackson and Sarah could comprehend what they had witnessed. Time itself seemed to have stopped as they saw the dark shape as it was flung out of the window of the top story of the building. It appeared to hang in mid-air for a moment before it plunged to the ground, mere feet from where they were standing. The shape crashed with a wet thud, and Jackson could hear the air being forced from the lungs.

He and Sarah stared at the body, then at one another, both unable to speak before they turned back to the prone form. In the darkness, they were unable to discern any of the facial features or the gender or even the clothing it wore. Cautiously, they edged closer, listening intently for any sounds.

There were none.

Jackson aimed his flashlight at the window from which the body had been expelled, seeing nothing there, no face looking out at him from the gloom beyond. All he could see was the broken window, nothing else.

While he continued to study the building, Sarah stepped forward, shining her light upon the body, moving the light upward to the face. There was so much blood that she was still unable to identify it. As she drew closer, she dropped to her knees in the dirt to get a better view. When it hit her, she inhaled sharply and shot her hand out to grip Jackson's arm tightly.

He swung toward her, her hand upon his arm like a vise. "What is it?" he asked, still unnerved and frightened by what had happened.

"Jay," she whispered, holding back a sob that wanted to tear through her throat. She worked to clear the lump. "It's Jay."

Jackson's stomach turned to water, his knees grew weak. He dropped to his knees beside her, now training his light as well onto Jay's ruined face. Blood, so much blood. Too much blood. Too much blood for him to still be alive. Sarah moved her fingers to Jay's wrist, checking for a pulse. She found nothing. Frustrated, she moved her fingers to his neck. Her fingers smeared long, pale strips on the skin coated with warm blood, and were unable to find any sign of life. As she began to draw her hand back from him, her fingers felt the tear in his flesh, the hole torn into his throat which had sealed his fate, and she began to weep.

Jackson moved the light down the body, seeing the odd angle of his legs and arms from the impact. He looked back again toward his friend's face, the man who had been one of his first friends at college. He and Jay had spent more hours together than they had spent in classes while still in school. Afternoons of playing football on campus, weekends of drinking in their respective apartments, concerts spent tailgating during summers. All of it now only memories, never again to be a reminiscing conversation over new beers or while experiencing new things. All in the past tense. Like Jay. Jay was now past tense, too.

He was going to be sick. Jackson staved off the hot rush of acid from coming up long enough to turn away and move toward a small, scrubby bush alongside the building. He threw up quickly, violently, into the grass, bent forward with his hands upon his knees for support. Vomit came again, his chest heaving with the force of it. Saliva filled his mouth with an oily residue and the feel of it made him retch once more. He hoped he had enough water left in his pack to at least rinse the foulness from his mouth. He could hear Sarah crying softly behind him, still bent over Jay's body.

What the fuck were they going to do? How had this even happened? There was no one in that window. No one. Unless they had run like hell away from it…but where were they now? Were they still hiding inside the morgue? Were they waiting to ambush him and Sarah?

That notion made him move, made him forget about his stomach, which was still bent on mutiny. It would have to wait. Right now, he needed to get Sarah to relative safety and they needed to make a plan. They needed to do something.

"Sarah," he wheezed, turning back to her, wiping his mouth idly with the back of his hand. "We need to get out of here. It's not safe."

"But Jay…"

"We can't help him now, Sarah," Jackson told her as gently as he could, but with a sense of urgency to his voice. "Right now, we need to get away from here."

"Why?" she asked stupidly, not looking at him. She had moved to cradle Jay's head in her lap, her tears falling from her cheeks into his open and unseeing eyes. That sight in his flashlight beam nearly made Jackson start throwing up again.

"Because Jay didn't throw himself out that window, Sarah. He didn't do that to his face or to his neck. Someone else did that, Sarah. Someone else. And that someone else is…still…out…here." He whispered these words through gritted teeth both for quiet and for emphasis. "We need to move. Now."

"What about the others?"

Jackson, reaching his hand out for her, stammered. "We'll figure out something. But for right now, you and I have to get the fuck out of here. Before whoever did this decides to come for us. Understand?"

She nodded slowly, still too shell-shocked to fully comprehend the situation in which they had found themselves. Sarah took Jackson's outstretched hand and allowed herself to be yanked to her feet. Jackson extinguished both flashlights and pulled Sarah closer to him, tucking her into the crook of his arm and began to move with her, dragging her along to keep pace. The two of them moved in the direction Jackson believed Building 51 to be, heading back to a place he thought they could hide for a little while, out of sight, and hopefully find Georgia and Adam. If they were still in there, they were more than likely pissed as hell.

"Keep moving, Sarah, we have to keep moving," he grunted, tripping over a rock and feeling his ankle twist painfully. He ignored it and kept heading toward the big building he hoped like hell they were getting closer to.

She continued to cry as they moved, sniffling and uttering the occasional full sob, her chest hitching from the effort. "Try to stay quiet," Jackson urged.

"But I can't see, Jackson," she wailed, though at a lower volume than she wanted. The moon, which had previously lit the grounds, had moved behind a group of clouds and everything had grown dark.

"I know you can't," he told her. "I can't either. But if there's someone out there who is apparently killing people, I don't want him to be able to find us. And if we have the flashlights on, we'll be as good as dead."

He felt her nod beneath his arm and heard her crying begin to taper off as her mind was wrapping tighter around their reality. Empty buildings stood around them, open doorways like gaping maws that wanted to swallow them. What had been merely creepy in daylight was sinister in the dark, made more so by the fear enveloping both of them. The white trim around windows gave them the appearance of the whites of eyes, as if they were all looking, all watching as they traipsed through the tall grass and through the broken chunks of asphalt toward an uncertain destination.

Jackson felt himself begin to hyperventilate and had to slow his pace and slow his breathing. He counted to five for each inhale and exhale as best as he could while continuing to move at a pace somewhere between a walk and a jog. The panic was taking hold and he had to stop it in its tracks before he was completely useless to himself and Sarah and, for all intents and purposes, to the rest of their friends as well. They needed to find somewhere to hole up and make a plan and they needed to do it now.

He looked to his left and saw a few squat buildings they had passed earlier in the day. He had no idea what purpose they had served originally but all the doors and windows were gone and he didn't like the looks of them at all. No good. Had to keep going. They had to get to Building 51. There were enough wings and corridors there to hide themselves.

The seconds felt interminable. The minutes were agony. Finally, blessedly, Jackson saw the outline of Building 51 beginning to loom in front of them and he nearly cried with relief. "Come on," he grunted, urging Sarah on the last few hundred feet toward the doors they'd entered what seemed to be days earlier. "We're almost there."

CHAPTER TWENTY-SEVEN

Gregory had moved on from the cell his grandmother had once called home after simply standing in the center of it for the better part of half an hour, trying to will her to come to him. After awhile, he began to feel silly, just standing in the center of the ramshackle room. He had stepped back into the hallway, exploring the rest of the rooms of that wing. Now that he was alone in the building, he found he actually preferred it. He was no longer subjected to the occasional heavy sighs of exasperation from Sarah or Jackson rolling his eyes surreptitiously. They thought he hadn't noticed their behavior. But he had. He had seen it all, heard it all.

He wasn't so much mad that Sarah had left him there, but more that she had left with Jackson. That smug son of a bitch had never liked that he and Sarah were dating, had never liked him because he had replaced Jackson. And now he was trying to move into his territory, trying to undermine him to get Sarah back. Well, if she was going to be a whiner and complain about being here, maybe he would be better off on his own after all. She was forever whining that he didn't like her friends. That was actually true. He didn't. He had tried to play nice but today's trip had opened his eyes to how truly banal they all were. He sniffed, jutted his chin out in defiance, and kicked at an old soda can before him in the hallway, listening to it careen down the linoleum.

There was another sound behind him, a rattling of metal, a squeak. It sounded similar to the movement of a wheelchair, its wheels disused and protesting the motion. He jerked his head in the direction of the noise, but saw nothing in the gloom at the opposite end. He chalked it up to rats or an echo and moved on.

Ryon Hall, while completely ransacked, was physically in better shape than the others he had been in earlier in certain areas. There was less of the peeling paint and plaster, fewer hanging and broken lights from the ceiling. Garbage and abandoned equipment was everywhere, but this part of the building did not have the look of decay the others had possessed. The walls on this floor were dull beige with a filthy rose color on the bottom half. While still old, more time had been spent modernizing it than the other buildings he had explored.

Every room he glanced into, shining his flashlight around the perimeter, was full of something, each room different. One room held an army of ancient dot matrix printers, the type which held paper with holes on each side, fed through on a loop. Gregory didn't think he'd ever actually used one of those, but he had heard of them and was able to recognize it on sight. Another room held a number of fake leather chairs, more than likely used for some sort of exam or therapy. The faux leather was the same dirty rose color as the walls of the hallway and many of the rooms. He scoffed at the notion that the color was more than likely chosen on purpose, with the laughable belief that it would be calming to the patients. Ridiculous.

The room ahead of him must have been an examination room at some point. It was jammed with small tables and rolling carts still holding old medical equipment. He stepped into this room, taking a closer look at the machines. There was an electroencephalograph, the needles used to mark brainwaves long dormant. There were scales and other machines he was unable to identify. He wondered, not for the first time, if the state had added up the individual cost of all of the machines, furniture and other equipment left here, how big of a fortune it would have been. He couldn't even grasp what the number would have been, and he had only entered a fraction of the buildings housed in the complex. It was wasteful and shameful and should be an embarrassment.

He stepped back out in the hall, shining the light farther down. For a moment, he thought he saw someone stepping into one of the rooms just out of the reach of his flashlight, but he knew better. He was alone here. Jackson and Sarah were long gone on their search for the rest of their whiny friends.

Sure what he had seen was merely a trick of the light and shadows, he walked on. The next room gave him a bit of a start. He was unprepared for its contents; two mattresses on the floor, blankets and pillows on both. He moved into the room and probed the blanket on the mattress closest to him with his toe. There were even sheets on it. People were living in this building. Why?

On a small table between the mattresses were empty iced tea bottles and a canister of wet wipes. Across the room, upon a rolling cart being used as a table, was a jar of peanut butter. The idea that there were people who slept here regularly gave him the creeps. This was the first time he had been unsettled since setting foot on the property. Who would choose to sleep in a place like this voluntarily? Not him, that was for sure. If he had been homeless, he would have chosen someplace far less remote with far less chance of getting arrested for breaking in.

Gregory stepped back out with speed that surprised him, not wanting to spend another moment in someone's ad hoc bedroom. Walking through these abandoned buildings with their rooms long disused was one thing, but wandering into somewhere someone had slept after the state had moved people out did not appeal to him in the least. He swept his flashlight back and forth along the floor as he had seen security guards do in countless movies, barely acknowledging the piles of garbage strewn about haphazardly. Directly in front of him was a large stain on the linoleum, spanning almost the entire width of the hallway. It looked like blood.

As he peered around, he saw a similar stain in the doorway to the room ahead of him on his right. And then another a few doors farther down, and another. And another. What the hell had gone on in this building? Had someone been murdered? Could it be animal blood? Gregory could feel the hairs on the back of his neck rising in alarm. This went beyond the eerie bedroom he had seen moments ago. This was serious and potentially dangerous.

He slowed his pace, listening for any sounds out of place but heard nothing. Cautiously, he continued to make his way down the long hall toward the end, which turned to the right to another wing, its sally port barred doors open. No one left to keep in or out. A few steps ahead sat another rolling cart, made of old dingy metal and plastic laminate designed to look like wood. He wondered if that laminate ever fooled anyone. It was the basest imitation of wood grain at best.

Upon the table sat an empty gallon jug, similar in style to the large jug of white vinegar his mother always kept in the kitchen. As he approached it, he noticed the label was still affixed to the front. Betadine. He blew out a breath of relief. It hadn't been blood on the floor. It had been this. Some asshole must have found it somewhere in the building and thought, since the sterilization liquid was a dark and reddish color, it would be hilarious to pour it out on the floor to resemble bloodstains. Real goddamn funny. He shook his head in disgust and continued on, spirits lifted and confidence returning.

But only for a moment.

He heard a rustling in the room next to him, like papers shuffling on a desk. It was followed by footsteps, which were headed toward the hallway. Toward *him*.

Sufficiently spooked, Gregory took off toward the sally port and the other wing, not knowing what was inside the room and not wanting to find out, either.

CHAPTER TWENTY-EIGHT

Trying to be as silent as possible, Jackson led Sarah back to the door they had accessed Building 51 through earlier in the day. Had it only been earlier in the same day, only hours before? It seemed to have been weeks, months ago. The building which had seemed more sad than scary now felt menacing. He kept his pace slow in an attempt to mitigate the noise his footsteps created. They huddled just inside the doorway, finally taking a breath after their terrified journey.

"All right," Jackson whispered, "Do we text the others first or call 911? Do you want to do one and I'll do the other?"

Sarah looked up at him in the near pitch black vestibule, her face pale and her eyes wide. "I don't think I could have a real conversation with someone right now. Certainly not to explain what the fuck is going on here," she replied, her voice trembling, one ice cold hand still gripping Jackson's forearm.

"Fair enough," he agreed, nodding. "I'll call for help. As soon as I figure out what the fuck I'm going to say." He grimaced, and then began rummaging through his pack for his cell phone. Sarah pulled hers from her pants pocket and brought the screen to life.

Jackson did the same with his, the brightness of the phone's wallpaper hurting his eyes momentarily. He blew out a breath and began to dial, his fingers tapping out each of the three numbers and activated the call, bringing the phone up to his ear.

After a few brief seconds, he lowered the phone and looked at the screen, really looking at it this time. When he'd turned it on, he had only given it a perfunctory glance as he dialed. Now, upon further inspection, after hitting the "end" button, he realized he had no signal. That couldn't be. They were in the woods, yes, but the city was just outside the grounds. There absolutely should be cellular service here. And yet, plain as day, the top of his phone display read "No Service".

"Fuck!" he exclaimed, though at a muted volume. Jackson turned to Sarah. "Any luck?"

She shook her head, not looking at him. She was busy staring at her own phone. "I've tried Georgia, Adam, Val and even Gregory. None of the messages have gone through. It keeps telling me the message failed to send. I don't seem to have any service. But how can I not have service?" Her mouth moved into a deep frown.

"I don't have any service either," he told her grimly. That made her look up. "So I can't get through to 911." He quickly thumbed to his texts and brought up the most recent one. The one he had thought he sent to Adam earlier. Bright red letters exclaimed *"Not delivered"*.

"So we can't get a hold of anyone else and there's no help coming," Sarah stated plainly, the reality of their situation sinking in.

"Exactly," Jackson concurred, putting his phone back to sleep and placing it back into his bag. It was useless at this point. It would only waste more time if he continued to mess with it. He knew he wouldn't be able to complete a call.

"What do we do?" Her eyes looked too large for her face, her chin trembling with the onset of tears.

Jackson wrapped an arm around her protectively, drawing her closer to him. "We left Adam and Georgia here. We'll start by looking for them, okay?"

"And what if we can't find them, Jackson? What if we look in this goddamn building and we can't find them? And even if we do, then what? We go back in search of Valerie and Gregory? And what if we can't find them? What the fuck are we supposed to do? We never even thought about the possibility of something like this happening or getting separated and lost. At no point did it occur to any of us that we wouldn't be able to use our fucking cell phones."

She was growing hysterical and she knew it. The situation was desperate, and becoming more so by the second. Sarah was unable to stop the fear from bubbling up in her throat and it was all she could do to keep the tears at bay. She wanted out of this place. Now.

"I don't know, Sarah. I just don't know. It never occurred to me either that we wouldn't have service here. And I certainly never thought there would be some kind of fucking maniac on the loose here killing people. I didn't know much of anything about this place at all. But I don't think I could just try to leave here without looking for the others. I don't think I could just leave them here, especially with whoever killed Jay roaming around the grounds."

"But like I said before, what if we can't find them? How long are we supposed to spend looking for them? Are we supposed to stay here until that sicko finds us, too? Because I've gotta tell you, I don't want to end up like Jay, broken and bleeding on the ground like that."

"I don't either, Sarah. But we can't just leave them here. They're our friends," he pleaded with her.

A tear rolled down her cheek. "I know that. I'm scared as hell, Jackson, and I don't know what to do."

"Me either. And I'm scared, too. I never in a million years could have imagined something like this, even with all the horror movies I've seen in my life. I can't even think straight enough to start following horror movie rules, either. But I can't in good conscience leave my friends here without trying to find them and give them a fighting chance to get out. We'll retrace our steps from where we left Adam and Georgia here earlier. If we don't find them after that, we'll move on to another building."

Sarah closed her eyes, inhaled and exhaled. "Jackson, there are more buildings here than we can count. This place is enormous. What chance do we have of finding anyone? I'm going to say our chances are about none."

Impatient now, Jackson was starting to lose his temper. "I don't know, damn it! But we have to try, don't we? Are you really suggesting that we just tuck tail and run and leave them here? What if this guy kills someone else? Can you live with yourself if you let that happen without even looking for them?"

"And what if he ends up finding us while we're looking for them, huh? What then, Jackson? We'll have died for fucking nothing, that's what." Sarah was growing angry now as well. He was surprised at her. He had thought they would have been on the same page to try to get their friends to safety as well as themselves after seeing what had happened to Jay. That did not appear to be the case. Self preservation was strong in Sarah.

"God damn it," he hissed. "What do you want to do then? Flip a fucking coin? Heads we look, tails we run?"

She stared at him. She was actually pondering the possibility. "It's not the worst idea you've had," she told him bluntly.

"This is insane. Completely insane. We are going to decide the potential fate of our friends by a coin toss. Are you for fucking real?"

"It's not just their potential fate, it's ours too, and you know it," she retorted. "Now, do you have a quarter or do I need to root through my backpack?"

CHAPTER TWENTY-NINE

Up or down? Which way to go now? Gregory hesitated on the stairs, contemplating which direction he wanted to head. He tried to catch his breath, which was coming far faster than he would have liked. He was beginning to start at shadows, acting like a scared little girl who was afraid of the dark.

Like his girlfriend had been.

The noises in the hall had more than likely been caused by some animal which had gotten into the building. It certainly wouldn't be the first time something like that had happened. He'd seen evidence of their mess in the other buildings. It was probably a pigeon or some other bird that had flown through one of the missing windows. He wasn't about to allow some stupid animal spook him.

Well, he'd already seen the downstairs, so unless he was planning to check out another building, there was little point in heading back down. No, instead he would head up to the next floor and see what there was to see there. If it was a carbon copy of this floor, then perhaps it would be time to seek out something else. Or maybe try to find Sarah and the others and head home. It was late and it was dark as hell, as they had mentioned before. He just hadn't been ready to leave. Maybe now they had all seen enough. It hadn't been terribly difficult to get onto the grounds so he wasn't excluding the possibility of another one in the future. Preferably alone. Or with his own friends, at the very least. People who would appreciate the history of the site and the information it had to offer. Not these asses he'd come with. He had learned his lesson. He probably wouldn't even take Sarah next time.

Flashlight off, he started up the stairs toward the third floor. The moonlight illuminated the stairwell enough so he could see without any aid, and he grasped the handrail as he ascended. No noises came from below, which was a relief. Whatever had been down there was staying put. Gregory was glad of it.

The landing for the third floor held a metal door, which been propped open with an old and rusting toolbox. The door itself was covered in graffiti, the words obscured by darkness. Gregory had little interest in deciphering its message anyway, so he opened the door and slipped through into another hallway.

He found it strange how one floor to the next could be so similar in design and yet so different in how it had fared over the years of neglect and abandonment. While the second floor had contained less of the peeling paint and appeared more intact in terms of aesthetics, the third floor could not have been more different. Here were the more familiar signs of neglect he had seen in the other buildings; the dirty floors, the paint coming off the walls in strips, plaster in dirty piles and light fixtures hanging from the ceiling. There were more of the same with the doors off the main hallway with the doors all standing open, but they did not appear to be patient cells as on the second floor. These appeared to be more along the lines of offices or examination rooms. The doors were fewer on this floor, the gaps in between them far larger than he had seen downstairs. Equipment and furniture were stored in the hall, some of it in the doorways keeping the doors propped open. Tables, chairs, rolling carts, wheelchairs, all of the same things that had been stored elsewhere in the different buildings. It was merely more of the same. He could not help but shake his head again at the hefty amount of money the state had simply walked away from when they had closed this facility. No attempt had been made to repurpose or sell any of the materials here, it had only been left where it had lived and abandoned.

Gregory began to creep forward down the hall, flashlight back on and sweeping the floor and the doorways. To his right, the first room he came upon puzzled him and he stepped closer for a better look. Once he had entered the doorway, he could see why it had appeared different than the others had. Inside, the floor was covered from wall to wall in books. Hundreds and hundreds of books. Their covers were filthy; their pages were swollen from water damage and exposure to the elements.

He probed the pile with the toe of his shoe, moving it closer to him so he could make out the title. "The Wonderful Wizard of Oz" by L. Frank Baum. The room must have served as some sort of lounge or library for the patients of Ryon Hall. Odd that all of the books had been stored away here – except not stored at all. They coated the floor, no bookcases or shelves remaining. It was merely a large room of books and nothing else. An avid reader himself, Gregory felt something akin to a sense of loss at the fate which had befallen all the stories lying upon the floor, never to be picked up and read again by anyone.

Moving on, he passed his light farther down the hallway. The glow reflected back at him off the glass inserts in the doors, the angle almost blinding him for a second. In that moment, there was a short burst of movement to his left toward the end of the hall, closer to the opposite staircase. Quickly pulling the light to the side to avoid any further glare, he searched the landscape before him for any further sign of movement or any sound of footfalls.

He heard nothing but slowed his pace when he began to move again. It had looked as though whatever had been at the opposite end had disappeared into the final door at the end, but he could not be sure. Walking forward, he still had the irritating bursts of light in front of his eyes from the flashlight reflection. He decided to move into another room, out of the direct line of sight of any other potential people in the hall until his vision returned to normal. He selected the open door to his left, which appeared to be an examination room.

An odd setup for the building, he thought to himself as he stepped through the entrance and moved toward the rear of the room to the windows. The placement of the rooms and their purposes almost seemed to be scattered. Perhaps that was due to overpopulation and need for different things during different eras. He considered the long history of the hospital itself, and from the research he had done initially, it had appeared that every year the hospital had requested more funding from the state due to influxes of more patients and overcrowding. There was a constant need for more money, more beds, and more services. So the lack of strict logical placement of rooms more than likely wouldn't have applied here. On the opposing walls of the rooms were cabinets, most of their drawers pulled out to varying degrees, some of them full of papers or medical supplies, some of them completely empty. The contents of many of them had been scattered onto the floor, pipettes and tongue depressors littering the linoleum. There was an old examination chair near the center of the room, having seen much better days.

Gregory trailed his fingers through the dusty buildup on the chair as he walked past, headed for the windows. There were two of them in the room, both wide and containing the familiar wire mesh he had seen in the majority of the other casements. The glass had been cracked and broken in the right corner but the one to his left was intact and clear enough to see through. He stepped to the windowsill on the left, dousing his light and looking out to the grounds, which were illuminated with ghostly moonlight. The trees outside of the main thoroughfare were all in shadow, but there was almost a college quad feel to the grounds before where he stood. Ancient pavement outlined the buildings with a small patch of green in the center, where a lone, darkened street lamp now stood.

It was difficult to discern many details through the windows due to the wire mesh between the panes. The wire coupled with the late hour and darkness made it frustrating for Gregory. He could only imagine what it had been like for the patients locked inside the building, able to only get a look at the outside world through the asylum equivalent of chicken wire. Those who had more self awareness must have felt subhuman to be kept under such conditions, like animals in a cage. In this building, however, the majority of the patients had been criminally insane and most of them violent, so the likelihood that they were lamenting the freedom to roam the grounds was slim. They would likely have had other thoughts occupying their minds.

Turning back from the window, he brushed the majority of the dust and dirt from the exam chair in the room. After inspecting it for a moment, he hoisted himself into it, leaning back gingerly into the headrest. Gregory closed his eyes, any thoughts of the strange movements in the hallway all but forgotten. He was visualizing what the building must have been like in its bustling heyday, when the wards were teeming with patients and orderlies, all attempting to coexist in as non-violent an atmosphere as possible, at least on the part of the hospital staff. It was doubtful the patients gave much thought to a peaceful atmosphere at all.

What had the typical day in the life of a resident of Ryon Hall been like, Gregory wondered to himself. Had it been full of injections of medication to merely keep them docile? What had it been like when his grandmother had been there, before the advent of the majority of the medications used now? What treatments or therapies had been used on her? Had she been able to find any sense of peace in her life after murdering her child? Had the staff punished her for her crime, apart from her sentence to the hospital for the rest of her days?

He imagined the walls of the building with fresh coats of paint, with gleaming floors after the maintenance staff had polished them overnight. Nurses in crisp white uniforms, their crepe-soled shoes whispering them up and down the hallways, orderlies in their own uniforms piloting dazed, wheelchair-bound patients into rooms for therapies or examinations or shepherding them to their own quarters to be separated safely from the herd.

Realizing the scene he was imagining was more along the lines of a mental health utopia instead of the terrible reality, he altered his mental image. The smell would more than likely have been terrible, given the propensity for patients to soil themselves, especially those who were heavily medicated and those who were most disturbed. The ambient sound would have been comprised of a symphony of crying, of screaming, of nonsensical mumbling. The combined effect of all of these details would have been a living nightmare, and one which the staff of the hospital voluntarily went to each day, working long, hard hours to endure with very little escape at the end of the day since much of the staff in the earlier years lived on the grounds.

Could he have endured that life? Gregory supposed that depended on any number of factors, greatest of which would have been which life? The life of a patient or that of the staff? Both seemed distasteful to him, if he were being honest.

Lying in the chair with his eyes firmly shut, firmly entrenched in his own imagination, Gregory could almost feel the hospital come to life around him. He could smell urine and feces with an undercurrent of something antiseptic and a hint of floor polish. He could hear groans and shouts and sobs surrounding him. The vinyl cushion beneath his hands felt smooth under his palms where his hands gripped the rests.

He snapped his eyes open in alarm. Keeping them closed had assisted in helping them adjust to the darkness. The room around him appeared just as it had when he had stepped into it. It was still a ruin of opened drawers and broken cabinets and detritus covering the floor. He wondered to himself why he had thought it wouldn't have appeared that way. The sounds and smells had disappeared, though Gregory was sure they must have only ever existed in his imagination.

Perhaps it was time to move on to another room. He rose from the chair and headed back to the hallway, flicking his flashlight to life and not daring to look back. His heart was trip-hammering in his chest and he stuffed the fear down. He was beginning to act like Sarah and her friends, afraid of shadows and things that only existed inside his mind. What things lurked in his mind, if he was really getting down to it? Was his mind anything like his grandmother's? She *had* belonged here, after all, in this building, the one reserved for the most insane, the most dangerous, the most resistant to rehabilitation. What did it say about him that he came from that genetic stock?

"Bullshit," he muttered gruffly, casting aside the notion there could possibly be anything wrong with him. That was utter rubbish and he knew it. Being in this place for so long was wearing on him. He was hungry and tired and had been wandering around for hours. He decided it was time to finish up this building and head home. Fuck the others. They could find their own way out.

CHAPTER THIRTY

Jackson had tried not to gloat too much when he won the coin toss but was not entirely successful. His good humor at winning disappeared quickly when he saw the look on Sarah's face, which was an expression of sheer terror. Every moment they remained on the property, her fear ratcheted up another notch that the same fate which had befallen Jay would be theirs as well.

Jackson reached out an arm, pulling Sarah closer to him and sighed. "All right. I know you're scared. So am I. How about this? We'll search this building and then we're out of here, okay? Whether we find anyone or not, after we get through here, we're done. We'll find our way back out by the power station and go back to the cars. All right? We'll get back to Louise's and we'll call the police and *they* can go find everyone else."

Sarah nodded gratefully. "Yes," she agreed, taking a moment to compose herself. "Where do we start?"

Jackson looked around; taking in the dark interior of the building they had seen earlier in the day. It appeared completely different in the pitch black of night. He chewed his lip as he contemplated her question.

"I'm not sure," he answered honestly. "Do you want to split up? We could cover more ground that way and would be done sooner."

Sarah cocked an eyebrow at him. "Have you learned nothing in your life, Jackson? No, we are not splitting up. That's incredibly stupid and I'm insulted you even mentioned it."

He raised his hands in a warding off gesture. "All right, all right, forget I said anything. We stick together, then."

"Like glue," Sarah affirmed. "Maybe we should start with where we left Adam and Georgia. Maybe they're still there, bored out of their minds."

Sarah followed him as he headed toward the back of the building, where they had found the entrance to the other wards and had last seen their friends.

As hard as he tried, Jackson was unable to recall the placement of furniture and other items left behind in the building from when they had traversed the area earlier. Every few minutes was met with a new outburst of swearing as he barked his limbs against another obstacle.

Sarah seemed to be faring better than he was and was trying not to laugh at him when he erupted in a fit of curses. His bulk was shifting everything out of her way and she stayed faithfully in his wake as they moved through the large entrance and then farther back into the opening to the wards.

After what felt like ages, they found themselves back in the glass enclosure where Adam had fallen and cut his hand open that afternoon. The pair stood for a moment in the glass tunnel, eyeing the ground suspiciously. They were afraid it would be more treacherous in the dark than it had been during daylight. Jackson hesitated before moving forward any further, looking out at the abandoned grounds visible through the glass. Nothing moved. All was silent.

"Slowly," he urged Sarah, grasping her hand as he edged forward through the tunnel. "Watch out for the moss. That's what Adam slipped on."

"I know," she hissed in response, but minded his cautionary instructions all the same. They stepped tentatively, testing each stone before placing their full weight upon it. Having seen the aftermath of Adam's injury, they were both panic stricken by a floor which, in daylight, would have taken them mere seconds to cross. Now it was a journey of at least five minutes as they refused to move with reckless abandon. They had seen firsthand the possibilities a simple slip and fall could result in here.

Jackson and Sarah both breathed a sigh of relief as they stepped over the threshold into the actual ward and out of the tunnel. They paused there, where they had left Adam and Georgia, to take stock. Neither of them heard anything and there was no sign of either of their friends.

"Where do you think they went?" Sarah asked, straining to looking farther down the hallway. There were no signs of flashlights in the distance or any movement.

He shrugged in response. "I really couldn't say," he admitted. "Maybe Adam felt better and they went exploring in the building? It was so long ago, who knows what the hell they decided to do. Hell, the sun was still up when we left here."

She nodded. "Good point. Knowing Georgia, she probably got bored after about five minutes. So even if Adam was in pain, I'm sure to appease her, he probably agreed to explore more in the building. This kind of thing was right up her alley, so I think we should check upstairs after we get through this long hall."

"I think you're right," Jackson agreed. "I'd imagine they had to have figured out that there was no cell reception. If they were bored, they'd have played around on their cell phones and as soon as they had no access to social media, probably started going through the building for something to do. Let's get moving then. The sooner we get through the building, the sooner we can go home."

"Right on," Sarah said, and followed Jackson down the long corridor toward the stairs to the upper floors of the patient wards.

They moved as silently as possible, which was made easier by the lack of objects littering this part of the building. Their shoes made the occasional squeak against the tile floor, at least in the parts where it was bare of garbage, but otherwise their progress was quiet. Jackson attempted to shield his flashlight in the hopes that it would be less noticeable from the outside, and showed Sarah how to do the same with hers. He didn't want to risk detection from anyone outside but there was precious little else to be done in the dead of night.

"What I wouldn't give for a set of night vision goggles," he muttered under his breath.

"What?" Sarah asked, straining to hear from behind him.

"Nothing, just thinking out loud," Jackson responded, continuing forward into the gloom.

They continued to the end of the hallway and were faced with a staircase. "We go up then," Jackson said. "I didn't see anything down here."

"Me either," Sarah agreed. "It's not like they left a trail of breadcrumbs, either."

Up they went. Jackson continued in the lead, up the flight of stairs. The door to the second floor of the ward was propped open, just as they had left it earlier. They stopped again to listen for any sounds of occupation and, hearing nothing, stepped through the doorway and into the hall.

"I keep expecting someone to jump out wielding a chainsaw," Jackson confessed, stepping farther out of the doorway.

"I can't say I haven't imagined the same thing," she agreed. "I just wish you hadn't mentioned it."

"Me too," he replied. "Come on. A chainsaw can't really sneak up on you, anyway."

They were both afraid to call out for their friends despite the fact that neither had any idea if they had been followed from the other building back to Building 51. They were unwilling to take the chance not knowing where the person who had killed Jay was or if that person had any friends on the grounds. They had no idea what or who they were dealing with in this situation. The gravity of it was hitting them harder than when they had discovered they were unable to call for help.

Panic was gripping Sarah and Jackson both and they were at least grateful for the company of the other. Sarah was thankful to be with Jackson and not with Gregory. She couldn't imagine what his reaction would have been to the situation; probably skepticism and snark, neither of which would have been helpful. Jackson, similarly, was glad that Sarah was with him and that she was, at least for now, safe. It wasn't that he was unconcerned for his friends, he was, but Sarah's safety was paramount to him.

They swept each room they passed with their flashlights, realizing this action was keeping their progress to a crawl. They'd turned toward the wing on their right when they'd entered the floor and were slowly nearing the end of the hall. There were two rooms remaining before the wing dead ended. Jackson took the room nearest him and motioned for Sarah to take the one closer to her. He stepped inside, shining his light at the interior just as he had all of the others, with no results.

He went rigid when Sarah screamed from inside the room across the hall.

CHAPTER THIRTY-ONE

Jackson was at her side in a flash, clapping a hand over her mouth before she could utter another sound. "It's just me," he breathed into her ear. "Don't scream again. We don't want him to find us." He could feel her chest heaving, sobs wracking her body. Her mouth was moving beneath his hand; not in screams but like she was hyperventilating.

He turned to look at her, removing his hand from over her mouth. Sarah's eyes were wide with terror, fixed on a sight before her. He followed her gaze to the center of the room, where a figure was seated in a chair. The room was bare apart from that one piece of furniture.

"What the hell?" he whispered, stepping closer to get a better view. Sarah grabbed his arm and held him still. Instead, she pointed her flashlight at the figure to illuminate it for him.

"Adam," she whispered. "It's Adam." She began to cry again, quietly this time.

Jackson shone his light on the figure in an effort to better see what was before him. All the lights in the world could have turned on at that moment and it wouldn't have made the image make any more sense. How? Why?

Adam's lifeless body lay on the floor in the center of the room, tangled atop an old chair. His head was flung back, the top half of his face out of view. They had both recognized the clothes he had been wearing, along with the bandage on his wounded hand. They approached his body slowly, one agonizing step at a time. Rivers of dried blood coated his cheek. Protruding from his eye was a long, cylindrical piece of metal. His mouth was frozen in a silent scream

"Jesus. Jesus Christ," Jackson whimpered. Two of them. Two of them now were gone. What the fuck was happening?

"We have to get out of here," Sarah hissed. "Now."

Without speaking, Jackson nodded. He took her hand in his and the two of them began running back from where they'd come, no longer caring how much noise they made in the process. It was clear that Adam had been dead for quite a while. Jackson believed he was right to assume it was likely the same person who had thrown Jay from the building that had murdered Adam. Hopefully he was still behind them and they could make their exit without discovery.

They had been running for a few minutes when they both realized they should have reached the door to the stairs by now. Still moving, Jackson looked from side to side, trying to discern anything memorable in the dark.

"Did we come through here before?" he asked, out of breath.

"I don't know," Sarah answered, breathing just as heavily.

Jackson slowed his pace to get his bearings. Sarah kept moving beyond him. "Come on," she urged, turning back to look at him.

"Didn't we turn one corner too many?" he puzzled, putting his hands on his knees and bending over.

"I don't..." the rest of her sentence was lost as Sarah screamed yet again.

He turned to look, afraid the killer had found them in the building. But Sarah was gone.

Jogging forward, Jackson aimed his flashlight in the direction Sarah had been heading.

And saw the hole in the floor.

CHAPTER THIRTY-TWO

Gregory turned the corner back into the hallway from the examination room. There was one final door in the hallway. He decided to look inside and then he would end his exploration. Then it would be time to head back.

The hall was silent and dark, lit only by the dimming glow of his flashlight. He could not recall if he had packed spare batteries for it. The moonlight outside should be enough for him to find his way back to the hole in the fence near the power station. At this point, his eyes were adjusted rather well to the dark so he was confident he could find his way without incident.

The final door had no markings or identifying placards. As he drew closer, he could see a pale rectangle where a plate had once hung. It had long since fallen or been torn from its home. No matter. The door stood wide open and he stepped inside.

Within, his flashlight illuminated a large room painted in a light pink, and full of bathtubs. He realized this was the hydrotherapy room. Patients were kept in the water at all times, sometimes for up to a month. All of their meals were taken while engulfed in water, a canvas covering keeping them inside and immobile. Gregory had seen photographs of patients enduring the treatment with blindfolds over their eyes to give them fuller sensory deprivation.

It was a failed therapy, he knew, much like most of the others offered here. The occupational therapy, the act of creating rugs and dolls and shoes and attempting to give the patients a sense of purpose had been more free labor than it had succeeded in rehabilitating anyone under their care.

The bathtubs lined the perimeter of the room and several more filled the center. More of the graffiti "artists" had infiltrated this room at some point, spray painting the walls and the interior of the bathtubs. It was too dim to decipher the phrases inside of the tubs but one in particular on the wall caught his attention. *It was more fun in hell.* Charming.

He stepped inside, each footstep echoing. He noticed the bottom half of the walls had once been tiled, similar to a bathroom. Many of the tiles had fallen off but enough remained to cause the echoes he heard now.

Gregory stopped in the center of the room, staring. His imagination was working overtime again. Images of this room filled his mind. Walls back to a freshly painted state, white porcelain tile gleaming in the sunlight, and each bathtub occupied by a patient, the only part of their body visible their heads, emerging from the canvas cover over the tub. He wondered how they went to the bathroom when they were in there, then realized how distasteful the thought was and pushed it away. He could almost hear the sound of water running to fill one of the tubs in the rear of the room, nearest the windows.

Except that wasn't his imagination.

He *did* hear one of the tubs filling with water. That was impossible. There hadn't been running water in this building for years. He walked toward the sound slowly, not knowing whether to trust his own ears. It was distinct, the splash of water against the bottom, the rushing of it as it flowed from the faucet.

As he drew closer, he could see the glint of the moonlight reflecting off the surface. The water level was low, but was filling at a good pace. Behind him, he heard the rush of water coming from another faucet. Then another. And another. After a few seconds, all but a very few were filling as he stood paralyzed, watching in fascination.

What was happening? Was someone screwing with him? It had to be.

"You can come out now!" he shouted to the room, growing angry. This wasn't funny. None of it was funny. He was here for a serious reason. But all along, he had been the only person who had taken this trip seriously. Everyone else just thought of it as a lark, some dumb shit to do on a weekend for some laughs and excitement. He had been the only one with ties to the place, the only one with a purpose and these assholes were messing with him.

"Real funny, guys. You can turn it off, now." Anger flooded him, his face flushing in the dark.

He turned in a circle, seeing no one else in the room with him. It was only him and the bathtubs. The tub nearest him, at the window, had filled now and the water splashed over the side, soaking his shoes.

"Fuck!" he exclaimed, the water cold as ice on his feet. Walking back in wet shoes and soaked socks was not going to be fun. He hated the feeling of wet shoes.

"Where are you hiding? I've had enough of this shit. Nice trick but I'm leaving now. Stop hiding like a coward and come out already!"

"But darling," came a brittle voice from just behind him, warm breath tickling the hairs on the back of his neck. "I'm...right...here."

CHAPTER THIRTY-THREE

Louise had been sitting at her kitchen table for hours. The cup of tea she had made herself was ice cold and forgotten. Her hands were clasped in front of her, resting against her chin.

She had tried to go to sleep but it would not come. She had tossed and turned with the lights off to no avail. After that, she had flipped on the television, thinking it would provide a welcome distraction from worry. That effort had failed as well.

So now she found herself in the kitchen, terrycloth bathrobe belted securely around her, staring into space. Her mind was working furiously even if her body was still. She had been worried when Valerie had told her their plans. Louise hadn't liked it but she understood the draw of the hospital. They weren't the first group of kids to follow the siren song of an abandoned place, stuck in a snapshot of time, just waiting for someone to wander through it. She got that part. She just hadn't liked it. She had never liked that place, ever, even long before its closure.

There had always been stories. Stories when it was open of people going missing, of patients killed by the staff and each other, of staff killed by patients. Of overcrowding, of inhumane treatment, of experiments. The stories had given her nightmares as a girl.

After its closure, there were more stories. The screaming that went on at night long after the last patient had been transferred to another hospital. She had heard it herself from this very house. She had heard about balls of light chasing people, of doors opening and closing on their own. Several buildings had been lost to fire since it had closed, some of them started by lightning, some of them reported as arson. Sometimes she wondered if the fires were started by the buildings themselves in an effort to wipe their existence from the earth on their own.

The kids had been gone far too long. Their cars still sat in the driveway, their engines cold. She had initially thought that perhaps they would have just gotten in the cars and left, not coming in so as not to disturb her at a late hour. When she had given up on watching television, she had risen from her bed to check out the window. Their hulking shadows remained in the driveway.

She had come in here to the kitchen and made herself a cup of tea, which she never touched. For the last hour, she had been holding an internal debate with herself as to whether or not she should call the police. She didn't want the kids to get in trouble or get arrested. Hell, she didn't have the money to bail all of them out if that happened; she was on a fixed income.

But what if one of them had gotten hurt? She kept coming back to that question and getting stuck on it.

What if they couldn't make a call out? She wasn't sure cell service would be an issue or not. It was spotty at best here so it could go either way in the woods.

What if something worse than just getting hurt had happened to them? Those buildings were treacherous on a good day without feet treading on their rotting floors.

Anything could have happened.

"Damn it," she said to herself, and reached for the telephone.

CHAPTER THIRTY-FOUR

Jackson advanced mere inches at a time toward the cavernous void in the floor before him, uncertain how close he could get to the edge without risking falling through himself. Had this been here before or had Sarah triggered the collapse? He wasn't sure. He remembered there being a hole when they'd gone through the building earlier in the day but in the dark, he didn't recall where it had been.

The flooring ended abruptly, tiles having sheared off and fallen down below, rotted wooden support beams now exposed. He listened as he moved forward for any telltale groans or creaks in the floor beneath his feet. All was silent and he continued on, shining his light on the edge so he knew where to stop.

When he had gotten close enough to see over the edge to the floor below, he stopped moving. Aiming the flashlight down, he could see the debris from the collapse covering the floor. The light wasn't terribly strong, but performed well enough to see one of Sarah's arms poking out from under a pile of broken beams. It was streaked with bright, red blood.

If the hole had existed before today, Sarah had caused it to widen by running so hard over the weakened section of floor. It could have all given way. Jackson didn't know and didn't much care.

"Sarah!" he screamed, heedless now of the caution he'd used earlier to avoid detection. He didn't care; he had to get to her. There was no sound in response to his cry, no movement below him.

He needed to find his way back down to her, and fast. Turning around, he looked for a stairwell. His eyes probed the darkness, attempting to discern between doorways to rooms and doorways to a way down to her. After a minute's searching, he found the staircase they had come up; they had missed it in their panic after finding Adam's body.

Sprinting forward, he dashed into the stairwell and headed down as fast as his legs could safely carry him.

Upon reaching the first floor, he could see the pile of rubble in front of him, only a few yards away. Running ahead, he slid the last few feet, coming to a stop beside where Sarah's arm was protruding from the debris. Jackson screamed her name, over and over, as he began to pull pieces of wood and plaster and tile from the pile. If there was any reply, he did not hear it over his own yelling.

After a few minutes of frantic dismantling, Jackson was able to unearth Sarah's upper body. From the waist down she remained buried, but after a brief inspection, that seemed unimportant.

Her eyes were unblinking. Her mouth was frozen in mid scream and was full of dirt. He grabbed her arm with one hand, reaching over with the other to touch her face. There was no response at all, no turning of her head, no sound, and no resistance to her limbs. When he released her arm, it flopped back down beside her.

"Oh no," he breathed, utterly defeated. "Oh no no no no no no." The sobs came then, thick and hitching in his chest.

She couldn't be dead. Couldn't. He climbed astride the pile, kneeling before her. He placed his hands under her armpits and attempted to withdraw her body the rest of the way out from under its weight, to no avail. She was pinned underneath several beams and he was unable to move them on his own. She was trapped but there was no help for her now.

Her face was abraded and cut from the fall. While it hadn't been terribly far, the weight and violence of the collapse had been severe, more than likely breaking her neck and back when she landed.

She was gone and it was his fault.

If he had only listened to her and they had left when she proposed the idea, this wouldn't have happened. They could have been safely back to Louise's by now, on their way home, able to call for help to get the others out as well. But he had been stubborn. He had known best, or so he had thought at the time. He had to have it his way, just like always. And his way had gotten her killed. How could he ever forgive himself for this?

He caressed her cheek with his hand, wiping away at the dirt and dust upon her skin. Gently, he closed her eyelids and removed the debris from inside her mouth. He kissed her forehead, her skin still warm to the touch but cooling as each moment passed.

Jackson scuttled backward, crab walking off the pile until his back hit the solidity of the wall behind him and he could move no further. The concrete was cold against his skin, which was feverish from the exertion of trying to pull Sarah's body out. He sank against the wall, drawing his knees up and resting his head in his hands. The tears were still coming, hot and salty as they coursed down his cheeks, staining his shirt darker.

Sarah had been the first women he had ever truly loved. Jackson had dated in high school, as most boys did, and dated one or two girls during his first year of college, but those had only been casual. He had never taken any of them as seriously as he had Sarah. They had clicked from the very beginning, friends at first but the attraction had been too strong to ignore. His mind flooded with memories of their first dates, their first fights, the first time they had broken up. Many times over the years, heated arguments had occurred with an abundance of shouting and tears, from both sides. They would retreat to separate corners for a week or so and would inevitably find themselves back together yet again. After graduation, the idea of proposing had been on Jackson's mind, comfortable with the idea of spending his forever with her.

Until they had broken up that last time, an argument about their futures proving too divisive for them to come back together afterward. It had shattered him and for a time, he was unsure which direction was up and which was down. He had kept away not only from Sarah, but from their friends as well, licking his wounds and trying to put himself back together well enough to be around her and the rest of them. It had never registered that he could keep his friends without being around Sarah. That could never have been part of his reality. They were all entwined together, an entire unit, and it could not have existed without all of them.

When the time had come when he believed he had healed enough to enter the social world again, Sarah had found Gregory. And his spirit had been crushed all over again.

And now...now there was no future for her at all. Not with Gregory, not with him. She was gone. Her spirit, her fierce independence and loyalty...the way the light would shine off her red hair, the curve of her shoulder as it peeked out of a drooping sweater...all of these things were lost. What lay before him was only the shell of what she had been.

First Jay, then Adam, now Sarah. What about the rest of them? Val, Georgia...even Gregory. Where were they? Had they heard him screaming for her? He didn't even know if they had already left. What was he supposed to do? He couldn't call anyone. He wasn't sure he could find his way back out. Even if he could, could he seriously just abandon the bodies of his friend and his former girlfriend here to find help? Jay was still out there on the ground, broken and bloody after being thrown from the window. What would happen to his body by the time someone could get here to take him out? There had to be animals in the woods. What would they do to him?

What about the man who had been the one to throw him out of the window? Where was he? Was he looking for another victim? Had he moved on? He had to have been the one who had killed Adam. What was happening here? Was he searching for Jackson now? Surely his screams had to have been heard. His fear and panic had overtaken his previous urge to remain undetected and he had screamed for all he was worth when Sarah had disappeared into the hole in the floor.

He was probably headed straight for Jackson right now. And Jackson thought he may as well sit here and wait for him. He had gotten Sarah killed. Whatever fate befell him now, he had earned it in his arrogance and foolishness.

Jackson sat in the darkness and wept.

CHAPTER THIRTY-FIVE

Gregory jumped, turning in the direction of the voice that had whispered in his ear. He saw a skeletal old woman standing behind him. Her long, white hair hung in ropes over her shoulders, descending down to her elbows. She was dressed in a white nightgown which reached her ankles, showing wrinkled bare feet below the filthy ruffles at the base of the skirt.

His eyes were drawn back to her face. The cheeks were sunken, the skin almost paper thin over her skull. Her lips were ruby red, the only brightness in that pale, wizened face. Pale blue eyes blazed with insanity, focused directly upon him. One side of her head appeared concave, as if she had suffered a heavy blow.

She took another step toward him, moving closer until they were almost touching. Gregory instinctively took a step back, trying to maintain the distance. He recognized her from the pictures he had seen of her from before she had done…what she did.

"Grandma?" he asked tentatively, stepping back yet again.

The old woman smiled, and it was the most awful thing Gregory had ever seen in his life. She had a jack o'lantern mouth, jaw full of gaping holes where teeth had once been. The ones that remained were yellowed and loose in their sockets. The look in her eyes did not change, did not soften at the title. When she'd been committed, she had not been a grandmother and more than likely never knew she had become one.

One step forward from her. One step backward from him. They continued their strange dance until Gregory's heel struck the resistance of the legs of a bathtub. He was out of room to maneuver straight back. He stopped, evaluated his position. She was still a few paces away from him, his strides longer than hers had been. While he outweighed her by close to one hundred pounds and was easily six inches taller, he was still afraid.

Afraid because none of what was happening was possible. His earlier curiosity about the afterlife, the existence of the spirits of those once incarcerated here vanished and he knew only disbelief now. She had been dead for years. She had died here, long before any of the doors had been closed.

Yet here she stood.

Stepping toward him, reaching for him. Her feet made scraping sounds against the floor as she advanced, her nightgown trailing in the piles of dirt upon the floor. Gregory grasped the rim of the tub with his hands, turning his body to go around the curve of it and stand behind it. He began to back away yet again.

Had he really thought she would be unable to maneuver around the tub? If he had, he had been terribly naïve. She continued on, still grinning maniacally at him. Her small, horny feet splashed into the puddles of water on the floor near the tub, where it had overflowed. The water was still coursing from the faucet, spilling onto the floor of the room.

She couldn't actually be here. She was dead, buried before he had been born.

Then how to explain the crone advancing on him now?

"Grandma, I can help you," he told her, feeling stupid as he said it. "We can get you out of here. Would you like that? Or we can find one of the doctors to help you." Steadily he continued his backward trek toward the door to the room, toward the hall where he could make a mad dash for the staircase and the exit.

At the sound of the word 'doctor', his grandmother's expression became all the more horrible to see, twisting upon itself in a look of disgust and fear.

"Doctor," she spat, saliva flying from her mouth as she spoke. "Doctors don't help. Doctors just want to see what's going on inside your brain. Doctors just want to see what you look like on the inside. Don't want to help. Don't want to make me better." Her voice was awful, a mixture of a rattle and a little girl's voice, sing songy, which made Gregory's blood go cold.

"They told me I killed my baby. They told me I was bad. They told me I was crazy. That I could never be trusted around babies ever again. I never got to see my other baby. They locked me right up, locked me right up here forever. They poked around inside my head. They beat me when I didn't do what they wanted. They hit my legs, my back, so the important people wouldn't see all the marks." Still walking toward him, he still headed away from her. "But they knew. They always knew. They turned their heads so they wouldn't see. They closed their eyes so they couldn't look. I don't want a doctor. Maybe if I hadn't had doctors I would have gotten to be with my family again. Maybe if I hadn't had another doctor, I wouldn't have spent my whole life here…in hell!"

She lunged for him then, and he leapt backward. In his haste to get away, he slammed into a forgotten bathtub. He had jumped back into it, the hard ridge striking him across his lower back, stunning him. Gregory fell backward, splashing into the cold water. He was folded in half, legs hanging over the edge, his arms submerged. He flailed, trying to get his body to cooperate after the blow and pull himself out.

His grandmother was upon him, her thumbs in his eyes, fingers digging into the flesh at the back of his skull. She rocked his head off the back edge of the tub, howling like a banshee as she did so. Gregory cried out, bringing his hands up to try to pull her off him. His hands braceleted her wrists, yanking at them to get her fingers out of his eyes. There was so much pressure and pain as those small fingers dug into the soft skin around his eyes. Behind his eyelids were kaleidoscopic flashes of light as she continued to press harder.

He howled as loudly as she, the two of them a terrifying chorus, his voice full of terror, hers full of rage. She drew herself closer, increasing the pressure on his eyes, and pushing him to his right, until his face was below the water line.

As he felt the water rising over his face, he tried to stop his screaming but instead drew in a massive amount of water. Choking and sputtering, his reflexes only betrayed him further. He was unable to hold his breath, his lungs trying to force out the water which had gotten in, and in so doing, only drew in more.

His own body was killing him just as much as his own grandmother. He had been the one to bring them all to the hospital, his own curiosity what had taken them all through the hospital grounds. His determination to find out more about the woman from whom he was descended was now to be the cause of his own end.

When his lungs were no longer full of air and only of water, his body spasmed a few times more, then lay still, his face distorted under the ripple of the still running water at the surface. Deep gouges at his eye sockets dribbled blood which bloomed in the water, red tendrils turning the water to a light, then darker, shade of pink.

Hands released his head from their deadly grasp, and then withered away into nothing. Gregory was again alone in the room. The flow of water into the tubs slowed, then came to a full stop. The only sound was the occasional *plop!* as a remaining dropped pooled at the mouth of the faucet then fell into the water below.

No movement came from the tub in which he lay. The water was still, silent. His arms floated at the surface of the water, his legs hanging over the rim of the bathtub.

Gregory had gotten his answer, in the end. His grandmother was still there. She was still there, and she was still angry.

CHAPTER THIRTY-SIX

Louise followed the swirling red and blue lights as a new wave of responders headed up the old main drive up to the hospital.

Her call to 911 had not gone as she'd imagined it would. While she had expected some skepticism and resistance to sending anyone to check on the kids, she hadn't planned on the operator basically outright refusing to send anyone. Since Louise had no proof they were still there or that anything nefarious had gone on, the operator she spoke with recommended she just wait it out for the delinquents to finish up their excursion. The operator insinuated it was more than likely full of sex, drugs and vandalism and they'd surely show back up in the morning.

Unsatisfied with that response, she pursued her demand that they send someone out to look for them. It had taken some yelling and cajoling but she had kept her temper and refrained from cursing. Eventually, the operator had conceded and told Louise she'd send one unit to the scene to have a look around. Grateful, Louise had ended the call and placed the phone back on the dining room table with trembling hands.

She reached for her tea cup and felt how cold the china was to the touch. All there was to do now was wait. Alone. In silence.

She rose from her chair and headed to her room, changing into jeans and a sweatshirt, tossing her bathrobe and pajamas onto her bed. She was no longer drowsy; she was energized and felt a need to act. She could not sit at home and wait for someone to eventually either come home or have someone call her with an update. Instead, she went straight out to her own car, thankfully not blocked in the driveway, and headed toward the old main entrance. If the police hadn't gone there, she planned to check the other locations afterward.

But it seemed they had entered through there. The old main entrance was as sad and crooked as the rest of the place must be, Louise thought to herself. Once it had been a winding road headed up into the woods with two brick lampposts at the base. The posts had seen far better days, their surfaces faded and worn with time and exposure. She drove past this every day. Most of the time it never garnered any of her attention. The field was overgrown that led down to the highway. The grand home which had belonged to sitting administrators had burned years before and sat as a charred shell for all to see.

Tonight, the old house was hidden by the darkness and her mind was elsewhere. If any of the police gave her a hard time, well, she'd give them a piece of her mind. That was her granddaughter stuck up there somewhere. She'd be damned if she'd leave here without Val or she'd know the reason why. Old or not, Louise was not a woman to be trifled with. Her car wound around the drive as she ascended toward the top of the hill and the main building. She was thankful for the extremely bright headlights her car possessed as there was precious little light around her. The woods were dark; the street lamps which were posted along the roadways at the hospital dormant. She'd have given her eye teeth for them to be working tonight. The police would have a hell of a time finding anyone here in the dark.

She continued accelerating as her car crested the hill and came to Building 51. Police cars swarmed the drive in front of the building, lights flashing. Groups of men were gathered together in front of the building. One of the policemen approached the group, trying to maneuver what Louise assumed must be a bundle of rolled maps.

Pulling up to a small clearing not filled with official vehicles, Louise pulled in and put the car in park. She stayed seated, only removing her seatbelt, and surveyed the scene before her. The large group standing in front of one of the police cars was listening intently to one man standing before them as he spoke, apparently giving orders. Louise estimated there to be about fifteen men listening and taking direction.

If there were multiple cars here, they had to have found something. And chances were, whatever it was wasn't good. The operator had told her *one* unit would be sent. This...this was definitely more than one unit. One of the vehicles had K-9 stenciled on it. "Good Christ, what is going on?" she whispered.

Louise opened her door and stepped out into the chilly night. She was glad she'd chosen a sweatshirt. While the day had been warm, the night was decidedly not. Louise slammed the door shut, jamming her keys into the pocket of her jeans. Someone would have answers and she was going to find that person.

Gravel crunched underneath her sneakers as she trudged toward the group of policemen. There was one officer standing at the edge of the gathering who looked as though he would have rather been anywhere else. He was older and his eyes had a glazed cast to them. Louise approached him, thinking he would be quick to send her on to someone else and hopefully it would be someone who could help.

It took a minute for him to notice that she was there, standing on the edge of his periphery. She had to speak before he became aware of her presence.

"Excuse me, Officer," she began, measuring her words to remain calm while her heart was hammering in her chest from worry.

The officer jumped back, startled. He recovered quickly. "Ma'am, what are you doing here? Are you aware this is private property, in the middle of the night, in a no trespassing area and is a police matter?"

He was all officious arrogance and Louise didn't like that one bit. "Yes, I'm aware of all of those things," she replied, glancing at his nametag. "Officer Foley, I'm here because I'm the one who called 911."

He nodded. "So then you can see that we've taken the call seriously and are looking into it, just as I'm sure the operator must have told you."

"Not exactly," Louise countered. "The operator told me that they would send one unit here. *One*. This is not one unit. So I would like to know what's going on."

Foley frowned at her. "Ma'am, if the operator told you they were sending someone out here, why are you here?"

"Look. I called for help because a group of kids, well, they aren't kids but they're kids to me, left to come here over twelve hours ago. I know they haven't come back yet because their cars are all in my driveway. This is the same information I gave to the operator! One of those kids is my granddaughter. Now, you tell me – if your daughter or granddaughter had left your house *more than twelve hours ago* to go exploring somewhere and hadn't come back and 911 told you to just 'sit tight', what would you do? Would you sit at home and wait for someone to call you?"

He thought a moment before answering. "No, ma'am, I don't suppose I would," he agreed solemnly. "I'm not encouraging you to stay. In fact, I'm encouraging you to do what the dispatcher told you." Louise began to bristle at this. "But since I'm relatively certain you aren't going to listen to that advice, I will say that you need to stay out of the way. I would suggest you wait in your car."

"But what is happening? I said before, they told me one car. Why are you all here? What did you find? *Where is my granddaughter?*" She felt instantly faint, and angry, and desperate for information.

Foley chose his words carefully when he answered her. He reached out his hands to grasp Louise's arms at the elbows. "Take it easy. What's your name, ma'am?"

"Louise. Louise Hood."

"All right. Now, Mrs. Hood, we don't know much yet, we haven't been here that long. And if you've lived in this area as long as I have, you know that this site is huge and it's going to take some time to search it and there's no power."

"But why are there so many of you now? *What did you find?*" she pleaded, her voice raised to near shouting. She was panic stricken and desperate.

He gripped her arms tighter. "It looks like…it looks like there's been an accident and someone got hurt. One of the floors in the building collapsed and one of the kids fell through. There's another kid in there as well, but he didn't fall through the floor." His tone was calm, soothing, trying to keep from frightening the old woman further.

"Who? Who were they? Where are they now?" Louise looked around, straining for a glimpse of Val or her friends.

"I can't tell you that right now, Mrs. Hood," Foley replied, continuing to employ the calm voice. "What's your granddaughter's name?"

"Valerie. Her name is Valerie," she stammered in reply.

"All right. I *can* tell you that it wasn't Valerie who was in that accident in this building. I can't tell you much else other than we are still looking for the others. That's why we called in more people, to search. So let us do our job, Mrs. Hood. If you insist on staying, for now I'll let you, but you have got to stay in your car. Can you do that?"

Louise nodded, gray hair bobbing with the motion. She didn't know whether to feel more afraid or feel some relief. She thanked the officer meekly and retreated back to her car, sliding back into the driver's seat, curling her body and drawing her legs up to watch the activity out the window.

The group of officers that had been gathered near Officer Foley disbanded shortly after Louise had gotten back into the car, all of them headed off in pairs in different directions, their flashlights out and at the ready. A few remained at Building 51, stationed outside the building. Louise thought there had to be more of them inside the building. It was vast and winding and she didn't think the whole thing could have been searched already.

She looked out toward the building, which loomed over her like a specter. God, she hated this place. Nothing good had ever come out of this place. Just let them be okay, she thought to herself. Foley had said there'd been an accident. He hadn't said that anyone was dead, just an accident. She couldn't help the feeling of guilt that flooded through her. They had left their cars at her house. She had known where they were going and she hadn't stopped them. Could she have stopped them, if she'd really tried? Probably not, no. But the guilt was there, knowing where they'd gone and waiting as long as she had to call for help. What if she had called earlier? Would someone have found them before this accident had happened? Maybe. Maybe not.

She leaned her head against the back of her seat and shut her eyes, letting the anxiety and uncertainty flood through her. She shut her eyes and let it come instead of continuing to fight it.

CHAPTER THIRTY-SEVEN

Jackson roused at the group of flashlight beams shining in his face. He did not know how long he had been sitting with his back against the wall, but his stiff limbs told him it must have been a while. He attempted to rise from the ground but a flurry of shouts and his numb legs did not allow for it and he remained in the same position.

Shielding his eyes from the light, he looked ahead of him from where it had come to see several men moving toward him. It appeared help had finally arrived though he could not make sense of how they had found them. Regardless, they were welcome. "Help her!" he cried, pointing toward Sarah, despite knowing that help had come far too late for her.

One of the men reached him, stopping directly before him. He was in a police uniform, a grave expression on his face. He shone his light upon the rubble which encased Sarah. The officer did not offer or move to assist Jackson to his feet. Jackson saw that the hand not holding the flashlight was hovering over his holstered service weapon, which Jackson found puzzling. They all needed to get out of there before the killer found them.

"What happened here?" the officer asked, his eyes wavering between Jackson and Sarah's body.

"Officer, we have to get out of here. Have you found Georgia and Val and Gregory? Someone...someone killed Jay and Adam. Sarah and I were trying to hide from him. We tried to call for help and couldn't get a signal. We tried to hide, we tried to find the others and Sarah...she fell through the floor." His words spilled out in a rush. He felt like he wasn't making much sense but he didn't think the officers understood the urgency in leaving this awful place.

"What's your name?" one of the other officers asked, standing beside Sarah's body, bending over to inspect the site.

"Jackson. Jackson McAllister." He stammered his name out to them. Why were they not moving? Why where they taking their time and looking around the room? They needed to go. Now. "Officers, I think we should get out of here as soon as possible. I haven't seen him but I know he must be around here somewhere."

"Who?" a third officer asked, sounding like an owl as his voice echoed off the walls of the hallway.

"The killer!" Jackson exclaimed. "The guy who killed my friends! He's out there and I know he knows we're still here. We aren't safe here."

"Mr. McAllister, we have been all over the grounds tonight and the only living person we have seen since we got here is you."

"What are you talking about?" Jackson shouted, now rising to his feet from his position on the floor. "What about Georgia? What about Valerie?"

"Stay right where you are," the first officer instructed him, his hand no longer hovering above his weapon. Now his fingers were wrapped around it, his thumb upon the snap to free it from the holster. His voice was calm but firm. "How many of you were there?"

Jackson was so panic-stricken that he had to pause a moment to count in his head. "Seven. There are seven of us. Sarah, Gregory, Georgia, Adam, Jay, Valerie and me."

The officers all glanced at one another. The first one spoke again. "And you say that a man killed your friends."

"Yes."

"Can you describe this man to us?"

"I didn't see him. But I know he's out there."

"If you didn't see anyone, how do you know that someone is out there?" The second officer asked, sounding as if he was losing patience, and quickly.

"I just know," Jackson answered vehemently. "We. Are. Wasting. Time," Jackson urged through gritted teeth. "We aren't safe here. Can't we get out of here and then I'll tell you?"

The officer sighed. "We're policemen. There are three of us just in this room. If someone comes in, you can trust that we'll come out on top."

The officer standing near Jackson nodded almost to himself, his mouth set grimly. "Get up," he commanded, hand still securely on his gun. "Slowly. Stand up slowly. We're going to walk out of this building so the other officers can finish searching it. Then we're going to take you down to the station so we can continue this conversation."

Fear rippled through Jackson. "You think I did this," he said, unbelieving. "You think I killed my friends?"

"I'm not thinking anything, Mr. McAllister, other than we need to search the rest of the building. So get up now and we'll go down to the police station and you can tell me everything that you think happened here." The officer nodded again to his compatriots and they began to move in to flank Jackson as he drew himself to his feet.

"I didn't hurt anyone! I didn't do this! You have to get out of here before he comes back!" Jackson cried, the terror now rolling through him.

"We'll talk all about it, Mr. McAllister. Now, walk that way. Ahead of me. Slowly."

*   *   *

They installed Jackson inside an interrogation room and left him to wait. He was thankful they hadn't handcuffed him to the metal rings secured to the table but he was still terrified all the same. He was left alone with his thoughts, the fear for the rest of his friends, the despair for Sarah, and the terror of what was going to happen now.

It was more than an hour before anyone entered the room. There were two policemen Jackson had not yet seen. Both were easily in their late forties and that might have been a generous estimate. Neither were in uniform and, given the late hour, their clothes were rumpled and tired. One of them was carrying two steaming cups of coffee. He placed one before Jackson on the table. Jackson placed the cup between his frigid hands, trying desperately to warm himself.

"Mr. McAllister," the officer with the coffee began, seating himself across the table, skeptical brown eyes locked on Jackson's face, "I'm Lieutenant Bryant. This is Lieutenant Snider." The other man nodded in Jackson's direction and sat in the other chair opposite Jackson. "We're going to need you to take us through what happened out at the hospital tonight."

Jackson sighed and hung his head despite having known he was going to have to explain everything all over again. He clasped his hands tighter around the coffee cup and noticed how intensely he was being scrutinized by the policemen. He took a deep breath and began to explain. "My friends and I went to the hospital to check it out. It was Gregory's idea."

"Who's Gregory?" Bryant asked, sipping his coffee.

"He's Sarah's new boyfriend."

"Who was Sarah's old boyfriend? You?"

"Yes, but that doesn't matter," Jackson responded, watching as Snider began scribbling in a notebook he'd produced from his jacket pocket. "Gregory told us all he wanted to check the hospital out but he really only wanted to see the room where his grandmother had lived."

Snider paused his writing. "What?"

Jackson began again. "Gregory's grandmother. She was a patient at the hospital."

"Son, that hospital has been closed for years," Bryant explained, and Jackson interrupted him.

"I *know* that, sir, she apparently died there years ago. Gregory said he wanted to make contact with her. Said he wanted to make a Ouija board on the floor with spray paint."

The officers eyed one another. "A Ouija board, huh? Well, that's new."

"Trust me, Sarah and I thought it was a crazy idea and we both told him so. He didn't actually do it. I mean, I don't think he did. Sarah and I left him in Ryon Hall because we wanted to find our friends and go home."

"You left him there alone? And where were your friends?" Bryant asked, keeping the conversation going. He sipped his coffee, gaze fixed upon Jackson across the rim of the cup.

"Adam fell in the main building and cut his hand open. He and Georgia, his girlfriend, stayed behind while the rest of us went to check out other buildings. Then when we went to the morgue, Jay and Valerie stayed there to check out the upstairs because Gregory wanted to go to Ryon."

"So let me get this straight," Bryant said, shifting his weight in his chair. "Seven of you went in there because your ex-girlfriend's new boyfriend wanted to try to contact the spirit of his crazy dead grandmother and then someone got hurt and instead of leaving right then to get him some help, you all left them in an abandoned, condemned building to go check out another abandoned, condemned building, and then split off *again* to check out yet another abandoned, condemned building. Do I have that right?"

Jackson gritted his teeth. "Yes."

Bryant and Snider exchanged another look. "And then what?"

"Sarah and I left Gregory and went to find the others so we could go home. We went back to the morgue where we had left Valerie and Jay. Someone threw Jay out of a window. He couldn't have done that himself. Someone had to throw him."

A pause. "But you didn't see anyone."

"No! I saw Jay fall out of the window but it was dark and I didn't see who threw him. He was dead and we panicked and went back to Building 51 to find Adam and Georgia. Our phones wouldn't work. We couldn't text anyone, we couldn't call 911, and we didn't want to leave them there. When we got to the building, we found Adam upstairs. They were downstairs when we left them, but he was upstairs when we found him but Georgia wasn't there. Sarah and I tried to run out, to get out, and then the floor gave way under her." He began to cry, fat tears rolling down his cheeks.

The policeman before him pursed his lips, contemplating. It was a moment before anyone spoke. "Mr. McAllister, there is a lot of blood on your shirt. Is that your blood? Are you hurt?"

Jackson looked down, noticing for the first time that there was, in fact, blood on his shirt. "I don't think so, no," he answered truthfully, which felt like the wrong answer.

"Whose blood is that, then?"

"Sarah's," he replied. "I tried to help her. She fell when we were upstairs. I found my way down and tried to help her. She was already gone by the time I found her. I…I must have wiped my hands on my shirt."

"Is it anyone else's blood besides Sarah's?"

"I don't think so. I don't think I touched Jay after he fell, only Sarah touched him."

"All right. So Jay fell out of a window…"

"No, someone *threw* him out of a window."

"Okay. Someone threw Jay out of a window. Sarah fell through the floor. What happened to Adam? Tell me about Adam, Mr. McAllister."

Jackson let out a sigh. "I don't know what happened, really. We found him when we came back to this building to look for him and Georgia. He was in a room upstairs. Someone had…someone had stabbed something into his eye."

"So…you didn't actually see what happened to Adam, either."

"No, we found him upstairs in one of the rooms. But it had to have been the same man who killed Jay."

"How did it have to? You told me you didn't actually see anyone," Bryant said dryly.

"Who else could it have been?" Jackson asked, exasperated, his voice growing louder. He was frustrated, exhausted, and terrified. These men were supposed to be helping him and yet here they were, peppering him with pointless questions. Sarah's body was likely still lying in the pile of rubble, no help for her in sight. No one to take her out, clean her up. These men were no help at all. "Look, we trespassed. We broke in and were looking around. We weren't looking for trouble, we were just looking around and then someone started killing my friends. What happened to Georgia and Val? What about Gregory? Where are they?"

Grim silence for a moment. "They're dead. They're all dead," Snider replied, his voice flat and cold. "All but you."

CHAPTER THIRTY-EIGHT

Her head was pounding, a headache right behind her eyes. How long had she been asleep? It had felt like only a few minutes. It couldn't have been minutes. The sun was up, shining brightly into her eyes, making her squint. She had to have been asleep for hours.

She peered out of the open car window, surveying the scene. There was an ambulance parked outside the building. More police cars lined the road in front of the main building. A few officers milled around, radios squawking periodically with reports and updates from the men in the field, searching the grounds. Louise looked to find Foley, spotting him standing near the ambulance. His face was tired, grim. She looked around again at the officers walking by. They all had the same expression.

Feeling her gorge rise, her hands fumbled for the door handle. She exited the car and began moving toward the policeman. Her legs felt leaden, unsteady under her. A journey of ten feet felt like miles. As she approached, Foley turned his head and saw her headed his way. His expression changed, tightening.

"Mrs. Hood," he started, raising his hands in a warding off gesture. "You should get back into your car."

"Why?" she asked, her mouth full of dread that tasted like blood.

"Please, Mrs. Hood. Get back in your car. Go home. We'll send someone out to you as soon as we can."

"I'm not going anywhere until you tell me what's going on. Where's Valerie? Did you find her?" She was only a few paces from the officer.

"Ma'am…" Foley's voice was cautionary, warning her away. Away from what?

His radio crackled, a tinny voice emitting at high volume. "Bringing them out now."

Louise turned to the policeman. "Bringing who out? Did you find them? Are they all right?"

Foley sighed, shook his head.

Out of the corner of her eye, Louise noticed movement in the entrance to Building 51. Several uniformed men were coming through the doorway. Two of them led, dragging behind them a stretcher. The metal wheels clanged as they went down the stairs to the pavement, creating a jarring sound amongst the ambient noise of conversation and radio chatter. Two other men followed behind, pushing. She craned her neck to see who was upon it, but she couldn't see anyone.

As they drew closer, she saw the reason why. It was because the stretcher held a black bag. A body bag.

More noises drew her attention. A second set of people were coming out now, dragging behind them a second stretcher, its own black bag upon it.

Louise's hand rose to cover her mouth in horror and against the wave of vomit threatening to erupt. "Oh dear god," she moaned through her fingers, her eyes wide with horror. "Oh my god." She sank to her knees, Foley grasping for her and catching her around her armpits before he was able to bring her back to her feet and support her against him.

Foley had been on the force for twenty years and had never worked a scene quite like this one. Jaded he might be, but heartless he was not. He held Louise tight, not allowing her to fall to the ground though he sensed that was exactly what she wanted. To fall right to the ground, pass out, and wake up to this being all a dream. Except that it wasn't. None of it was.

"Are they all…are they all gone?" she asked finally, once she was sure, at least for the time being, that she was not going to throw up.

He grunted beside her. "Mrs. Hood, I shouldn't tell you any of this. It's an active investigation and we have to notify…"

"My ass. I'm her grandmother, god damn it. Is she dead? Are they all dead?" Her distress was palpable.

Sighing, he drew back from her and held her at arm's length as he had earlier. "All but one. We've found six bodies. I can't tell you more than that."

"Wait, one of them is still alive? Who?"

"A young man. Says his name is Jackson." Foley's eyes slid away from hers.

"Is he all right? How did this happen? Did part of a building collapse? I know that's happened before. Did they all die in a fall?" She was rambling and she knew it and couldn't stop herself.

"No, ma'am. I mean, yes, there was a collapse but…but not everyone was in this building. Some of them were in other buildings on the property."

"Well, what does Jackson say? What happened?"

Foley was still unwilling to completely meet her eyes. "He's not making a lot of sense. Keeps telling us there's a murderer here. That someone killed his friends. But he never saw anyone, can't give us a description. We're interviewing him. He'll be brought to the station shortly for further questioning. We'll, uh, need you to come down at some point as well so we can take your statement." Louise began to weep, uncontrollable sobs as she covered her face in her hands. Foley pulled her to him and held her until her tears subsided, which took a very, very long time.

Once she had herself back under control again, Foley saw her to her car to send her home. "Are you sure you're all right to drive, Mrs. Hood? I know it's not far but if you aren't feeling up to it, I can have an officer bring you back home."

She gave him a wan smile through her tears. "That's kind of you, and I do appreciate it. But no, I'll be fine. I'd say your officers have their work cut out for them. This old lady can drive herself."

Louise stepped back, leaning against her car, staring at the looming building in front of her. Emergency vehicles littered the road, their flashing lights turned off by this point. Most of them had been there for hours. She stared hard at the once grand brick façade, took in the fine attention to detail that had been paid when it was constructed so many years ago. She looked to the windows of the wings, barred and many of them broken, that so many countless broken people had stared out of at a world to which they did not belong.

"They should burn this fucking place to the ground," she muttered, more to herself than to Foley. "They should burn it down before it ruins any more lives. It's taken enough."

Foley watched her drive away, her car headed back down toward the highway, a plume of dust swirling in her wake. "Frankly, Mrs. Hood, you're probably right," he agreed, and turned to eye Building 51 suspiciously, feeling suddenly cold all over.

That evening, when the last car had left, the Hudson River State Hospital was returned to its previous state of quiet watchfulness. There was no movement on the grounds.

But inside, the shadows still moved restlessly, still moaned and cried against the darkness.

And now, there were new shadows that joined the throng.

Six of them, to be exact.

EPILOGUE

"Wait up, you guys," Jeremy huffed, hefting his backpack over his shoulder, water bottle slapping against his hip in the carrier his aunt had given him for his birthday.

Ian turned to look at him, cracking a smile. "Come on, slowpoke. We're not waiting around for you all day." He turned and headed into the tree line.

"Damn it," Jeremy said under his breath, quickening his pace. "You know, I wouldn't be so far behind if one of you jackasses had bothered to remember the camera was still in the car."

"Whatever, man!" Ian's voice sounded more distant as he continued on to catch up with the rest of them.

He could hear girlish laughter and Ian's version of witty banter, which was far from it. They had all had a couple of beers before they'd headed in, tailgating their expedition. Jeremy had drunk a few for some liquid courage. He hadn't been excited at the prospect of coming here but had been too sheepish to back out. He would never have lived it down. They had left their cars in the home improvement store parking lot, the shopping center butting up against the grounds. It offered the easiest, but also most obvious, access. In their youthful naïveté, they had decided on the laziest option, the one which almost confirmed they would be discovered.

Joanna and Liz were farther ahead, walking next to Ian. Jeremy closed the gap between them. "Are you guys sure you want to go in here?"

"Of course," Liz replied. "Don't you?"

"I heard there's a cop around at all times," Joanna said, sounding doubtful. "I don't really want to get arrested."

Ian rolled his eyes skeptically. "It's a *huge* place, Joanna. He can't be everywhere at once. If we see somebody, we hide. There's plenty of places around for that. I've been here before and I've never seen any cop. Met a couple of homeless people once but they don't bother anybody so long as you leave their shit alone."

Jeremy was still unnerved. "Yeah, but didn't you hear about the guy who killed all of his friends here?"

"What are you *talking* about, man?" Ian asked. While best friends, that didn't mean they weren't continually exasperated by one another.

"Two years ago. A bunch of people went here to explore, take pictures and shit. They all died. All but one of them. Cops say he killed them all. Went crazy and killed them all. Now he's locked up in one of these." Jeremy jerked his thumb toward the brick building which appeared on the horizon.

Joanna and Liz looked a little green at the suggestion. "Seriously?" Liz asked.

"I think I remember that," Joanna concurred. "He said there was a murderer that must have done it all. The cops didn't believe him."

"You guys really believe that shit?" he asked, laughing. "We'll be fine. Now, if you're all done being scared of your shadow, the way into Building 51 is up here."

The foursome walked forward, into the shadow of the waiting, silent building.

Acknowledgements

I've been driving past the Hudson River State Hospital ever since I can remember, its graffiti covered buildings standing tall against the sky on Route 9 as you head toward Hyde Park, New York from Poughkeepsie. Its tragic history and the uncertain future of the grounds have fascinated me. Along with my grandparents having been employed there and stories told to me by my father, it inspired me to write this book. I've tried to incorporate as much truth in its design and history as I could – while taking the obvious liberties here and there.

I would like to thank the following people for helping to bring Building 51 to life:

There were people who helped me to learn more about the Hudson River State Hospital and its history, namely my grandfather, Bill Ollivett, Fairview Fire Chief Chris Maeder, and Jack Whalen. My grandfather worked his wily magic to put me in touch with Chief Maeder, who was a tremendous help to me and also put me in touch with Captain Whalen. The Captain told me stories of growing up on the grounds and what life was like there for the staff. He sadly passed away in August of 2016 but is not forgotten.

I would also like to thank the wonderful women who operate the Hudson River State Hospital, who are the alumni from the Nursing School. Not only did they give us an amazing tour of the museum but they also dug out photos of my grandfather never before seen by my family.

Aaron – my sun and stars, for always being in my corner and supporting me;

Michael – for being my number one fan and telling anyone who will listen that his mom writes books;

Amber – for the early reads, the great notes in the margins, and the support;

Tami – for being sometimes more enthusiastic than I was about this story and for your amazing friendship;

Candace – you're a lifesaver;

My family and friends for their support and patience;

My birds – you know who you are;

And lastly, to my father, Sam, to whom I dedicated this book. Your stories helped make the hospital and its history come alive for me. Thank you for your support, for believing that I could do this, and for reading it before it was really ready. I hope this book wasn't too "chatty" for you. Thank you for everything, Dad. I couldn't be prouder to be your daughter.

About the author:

Jennifer L. Place has been writing for as long as she can remember - little snippets here, short stories there, awful teenage poetry, and novels. She has previously published three – *Second Chances, Letters to My Child,* and *Journey's End.*

Jennifer lives in the Hudson Valley region of New York with her husband, son, three cats, one dog, and a terribly large goldfish.